Deadly  es

A NOVEL

by

RUSSELL HILL

A Caravel Mystery
from Pleasure Boat Studio
New York

Deadly Negatives
by Russell Hill

ISBN 978-1-929355-84-6
Library of Congress Control Number: 2012931339

Design by Susan Ramundo
Cover by Laura Tolkow

Pleasure Boat Studio is a proud subscriber to the Green Press Initiative. This program encourages the use of 100% post-consumer recycled paper with environmentally friendly inks for all printing projects in an effort to reduce the book industry's economic and social impact. With the cooperation of our printing company, we are pleased to offer this book as a Green Press book.

Pleasure Boat Studio books are available through the following:
SPD (Small Press Distribution) Tel. 800-869-7553, Fax 510-524-0852
Partners/West Tel. 425-227-8486, Fax 425-204-2448
Baker & Taylor Tel. 800-775-1100, Fax 800-775-7480
Ingram Tel. 615-793-5000, Fax 615-287-5429
Amazon.com and **bn.com**

and through
PLEASURE BOAT STUDIO: A LITERARY PRESS
www.pleasureboatstudio.com
201 West 89th Street
New York, NY 10024

Contact **Jack Estes**
Fax: 888-810-5308
Email: pleasboat@nyc.rr.com

There is no such thing as inaccuracy in a photograph.
All photographs are accurate. None of them is the truth.

—RICHARD AVEDON

I had no idea that morning when I went into Bill Fosberg's camera shop that my life was about to be turned upside down. Fosberg's shop is a hole in the wall with dusty shelves, used cameras, film—an anachronism in a world of digital cameras and no film. Bill is ninety years old, or at least that's what he says he is. He was a street photographer for the old San Francisco *Call Bulletin* and during World War II he was a combat photographer in the South Pacific, and there's some shrapnel in his left leg that gives him a hippity-hop walk. But, Bill says, the trick is to die from the feet up, and he's as sharp as a tack, has all his wits, and if you bring an ancient camera in, he'll look at it and say, "I sold those in 1959. Not a bad camera, but a shitty lens. Supposed to be a Zeiss but it wasn't." And if it's stuck, he knows what to do: opens the back, uses the pencil from his pocket to poke something in the body of the camera, and suddenly the shutter works again.

I'm one of those people who still uses old-fashioned cameras with film in them. I do portraits—children, dogs, families— because there are still people who want a good black-and-white photograph. There's something classic that appeals to them. And that gives me the chance to do the other things I like to do: candid photos, street people, documentary.

Bill's shop is where I can get film and today I saw the Leica M3 in his case. The M3 was made between 1954 and 1966 and it wasn't just a new camera, it was an entire re-thinking of what a 35-mm camera should be. It was so advanced it took other camera companies years to catch up. A rangefinder, it had a bayonet mount, built-in frame lines for 50, 90 and 135 lenses. Parallax correction and a single non-rotating shutter-speed dial for both high and low speeds. There were other features, too, and it was the kind of camera that photographers still lusted after. The body was built like a tank.

"How much for the M3?" I asked.

Bill reached into the case and brought it out, placing it in my hands.

"For a dinosaur like you, three hundred bucks."

"Bill, I'm thirty-five years old. How can I be a dinosaur?"

"Because you're still shutting yourself in darkrooms, you smell like Dektol. And you know what a Leica M3 is."

"What would you give me for my Nikon SP?"

"A lot of grief."

"If I throw in that Minolta you repaired for me?"

"A shitload of grief. And twenty bucks."

"You'll sell both of them to some art student who's been told she has to learn to use film."

"That's right. I'm the only place left where they can find a camera that isn't digital."

"Where did you get this one?

"A friend died. His wife sold it to me."

"And you told her it was old and not worth much?"

"No. I told her it was worth $250 on the market and I would get three hundred from some idiot like you and I gave her a hundred and a half. She had some other stuff too."

"He was a photographer?"

"One of the best. Maybe the last of the best. Shit, they've all died off around me. I'm the last one left on the raft. You gonna buy this or just stand there bullshitting?"

"You've got a really nice sales manner about you, Bill."

"I'm ninety freaking years old. I don't have time for small talk."

I didn't need the M3 but it felt good in my hand and I remembered that Richard Avedon used an M3 when he did the Western America photos, so I said, "Could I make payments?"

"Sure," Bill said.

"How about if I paid in three installments, a hundred each month?"

"No," Bill said. "One payment. Three hundred smackers."

"Jesus, Bill, give me a break!"

"Do I look like a fucking bank, Michael?"

"For an old guy your vocabulary is a bit limited."

"When you get to ninety, kid, you can talk any fucking way you please. I'll give you twenty bucks for the SP and that piece of Minolta shit, so two hundred and eighty smackers means you get to walk out of here with a classic Leica."

"Nobody calls them smackers any more, Bill."

"You can call them dog turds if you like, kiddo, as long as the bank takes them."

"Did you ever have anything graceful about you, William?"

"A long time ago. My wife died in 1990 and she took all the grace with her."

I took out my checkbook and Bill laid a pen next to it.

"Anybody but you, Michael, and I'd insist on cash," he said, while I wrote out the check and handed it to him. He took it, tore it in half, and carefully shredded the pieces in half again. He dropped them on the counter.

"Bring the money in when you can. If you're lucky, I'll drop dead tomorrow and you'll be home free."

"Thanks, Bill," I said. I picked up the check fragments. "A hundred on Monday for sure."

"And you get this," he said as he reached into the case. He took out a slender box and set it on top of the counter. "The original box it came in. Some collector would sell his right nut for this. But you're a dinosaur. A thirty-five-year-old dinosaur. You'll put the fucking box on a shelf and load that puppy and go out and shoot with it."

I picked up the box and examined it. I had no idea that I was holding a ticking bomb in my hand.

"Whose camera was it, Bill?"

"Aaron Sturgis. He went to Korea in 1955 with that Leica. A twenty-year-old freelancer with no experience. He went off to shoot a war and he made history."

"How?"

"You go to the photo archives at the Museum of Modern Art and look up Sturgis and Korea and you'll see a photograph that made Mona Lisa look like paint-by-numbers. There's a soldier standing there and he's holding a boot in his hand, only somebody's ankle is rising out of that boot. He looks like he's the one who got shot, and all around him are bodies. The snow is falling and the bodies are dusted white and it's the most devastating war photograph anybody ever saw. I saw stuff in the South Pacific when I was there, terrible stuff. But nothing could match that Korean photograph. And it wasn't just good journalism: the black-and-white contrast, the framing of that teenage soldier, the heaviness of the sky—it was fucking brilliant, Mikey. He went on to do Viet Nam and Kosovo and African famines and Irish bombers."

"When did he die?"

"Last year. His wife brought his stuff in." He pointed at the Leica. "She said not to sell that to some rich collector. Sell it to someone who would shoot with it. You won the lottery, kid."

I put the camera in the box. It was an ordinary box that had Leica M3 printed on the top and a picture of the camera. It didn't look like a bomb.

Saturday morning I took the camera out of the box to load it. The manual was stuck in the bottom and I tapped the open box on the table to loosen it. The manual came out, and so did an oblong of cardboard that had been pasted inside the box. Along with the cardboard came a film sleeve with some negatives in it. Someone had hidden the negatives, sandwiched between the cardboard and the bottom of the box. I took them to the darkroom and laid them on my light table. They were 35mm negs and they weren't all from the same roll of film. A few were attached to each other, but some of them had been separated. There were seven of them, all black and white, an assortment that included some men standing in what looked like military combat uniforms, a landscape of some kind, and a woman sitting at a table.

I put the negative of the woman in the enlarger and turned it on. I focused it and brought it up to 8×10. She was leaning forward at a table, wearing a halter top, and I adjusted the focus until it was sharp. I turned off the enlarger, slid a sheet of paper into the frame, and set the timer. The contrast was crisp, and I gave it six seconds at f/16. I pulled the paper out and slipped it into the developer tray. As I watched, the blacks began to appear, gray at first, darkening. Her face rose in the fluid and I tipped the tray, letting the developer wash across the image to make sure the process was even. I lifted the paper, let the excess drip back into the tray, and dropped it into the stop bath. I agitated it carefully, moved it to the fixer, and, after a minute, turned the light on. The woman's face was stunning.

She wore a black halter top with a deep cleavage so that when she bent forward, elbows on the table, it revealed the soft curves and the narrow cleft between her small breasts. Her expression was intense and her eyes were wide and focused on the camera. Her dark hair fell forward, framing her face. One hand was pressed to the plane of her chest just below her throat, her fingers sliding under the fabric of the halter, as if she was absently stroking herself, quite unconscious of what she was doing. The other hand was at the side of her head, lifting her hair away from her cheek. There was a beauty about her that was evident, perhaps in the way her hand lifted to brush her hair back. She sat at an outdoor café table and the lettering on the window next to her was in French.

A single glass of white wine was in front of her. She looked as if she might be in her early twenties, but it was hard to tell. There was no doubt that she was a stunning beauty, not in the usual sense, but with an exotic and almost erotic presence.

On Monday morning I showed up at The Camera Shop.

"Mikey!" Bill crowed. "You brought me some money!"

I laid five twenty-dollar bills on the counter. "A hundred smackers, Bill."

"Nobody calls them *smackers* any more," Bill said with a cackle.

"Okay," I said. "Here's a hundred dog turds. And something else." I laid the manila envelope next to the money. "There was something in that Leica box."

"The manual." Bill said.

"More than that. There was a false bottom to it and underneath that were some negatives. And this was one of them."

I pulled out the photograph of the woman. Bill looked at it and let out a low whistle. "This was in there?" he said.

"You recognize her?"

"Jesus, eff-ing Christ," Bill said. He continued to stare at the photograph.

"I assume that means you do recognize her," I said.

"It's Emma. Early 1960's. Paris."

"Who's Emma?"

"Emma Sturgis. Aaron's wife. The woman who sold me the Leica." He looked up. "What were the other negatives?"

"Some guys in army uniforms., a landscape. I didn't pay much attention to them. This was the first one and I printed it and it looks like a Richard Avedon portrait, and I wanted you to tell me where it came from."

"Aaron Sturgis. I told you he was good, kid. Jesus," he said again. "Fucking Emma. There's more negs of her?"

"I don't think so."

"Well, for Christ's sake, go home and look at them! You mind if I keep this?"

"Be my guest. This Emma Sturgis. Would it be possible for me to meet her?"

"I'll ask. She'll probably be happy to meet a good-looking young man. Emma is the proverbial rolling stone. No moss on her!"

"How old is she?"

"In years? Late sixties. In spirit, maybe your age. She gets a look at you, you may need a stick to beat her off."

When I rolled my eyes, he added, "Emma collected men like you collect cameras. And she had champagne taste. Bring those negs in and let me see them. I should charge you another three hundred for them. Unpublished Aaron Sturgis negs. How the fuck did I miss those?"

I didn't get a chance to look at the negs. There was a phone message waiting for me when I got home. A woman's voice, well-modulated, a bit on the husky side.

"Bill Fosberg told me that you'd like to meet me. If you're free this afternoon between one and two, I'll be home. Buy a decent bottle of champagne on your way, will you? "It was followed by an address in Larkspur. I recognized it as one of the old houseboats that were moored along the wide creek that led to the bay. A boardwalk led out to them and they had all become a permanent part of the marsh, no longer floating as they once had. Some had been turned into little cottages, others still looked like the houseboats they once were. I looked at my watch. Quarter to one. I stopped at Ludwigs Liquors and bought a chilled bottle of champagne that I couldn't afford and was on the boardwalk that led to the address by one-thirty.

The woman who opened the door didn't look as if she were in her sixties. Her silver hair was cropped close and she was slim, with sharp cheekbones, and there was no doubt she was the woman who was in the photograph. She wore a pair of tight-fitting Levis, a white shirt with the top buttons unbuttoned, and a black onyx necklace and earrings. Her feet were bare and her toenails were a brilliant red.

"You're Michael," she said. She looked at the bottle I was carrying. "My kind of man."

"Isn't it a bit early to start drinking?" I said.

"You can drink champagne at dawn, dear boy."

The interior of the houseboat no longer looked like an ancient watercraft. It had white walls and teak flooring and the stern wall was all glass, looking out into the marsh. An egret stood at the edge of the water and the sun slanted in, casting a green glow on everything. The furniture was spare and expensive and there were several metal sculptures that looked familiar. On the walls were black-and-white photographs, one of them a match to the one I had left with Bill Fosberg.

She went into the galley kitchen and came back with two frosted champagne flutes. "Do the honors, handsome," she said.

I opened the champagne and filled the two glasses, handing one to her. She touched hers to mine. "To sex, food, and wine," she said. "Three things you should enjoy slowly and with passion."

"Bill warned me about you," I said.

"Bill never could keep his mouth shut."

I pointed to the photo of her on the wall. "The Leica you sold to Bill. In the box were some negatives. One of them was that photograph."

"So that's where it went," she said, sipping from her glass. "And you're the young man who's going to use Aaron's camera."

"Yes," I said. "It looks like it was used hard, but it's in great shape."

"Aaron took care of his equipment. That camera was one he covered several wars with. Even after everyone else was using big Nikons, Aaron stayed with that one."

"I don't remember him ever being associated with a wire service or a bureau like Reuters."

"He hated editors. Said he couldn't take orders. So he freelanced all his life."

"He must have done well," I said. I pointed to one of the slender bronze statues, a stick-like figure of a young woman. "That looks like a Giacometti. Is it?"

She nodded. "Aaron took some photos of Pablo Picasso's family. Picasso gave him a drawing as payment. Aaron traded that and some photographs of Alberto Giacometti's work to Alberto for those two pieces."

"How come I never heard your husband's name connected with photographing famous people?"

"Aaron never thought of himself as anything other than a journalist. He was happy when he was knee-deep in shit. He went places no one else would go. He said his mother had held him by the ankles and dipped him into the River Styx. 'I'll get killed by some kid with a pair of lawn shears, he used to say.'"

"It must have been exciting to be married to him."

"When I met him in Paris he was so goddamn handsome I had an orgasm just looking at him. And when he was home, wherever that was at the moment, it was like riding a rocket ship. But he was away most of the time. He went from one war zone to the next civil war."

"You have any kids?"

"One daughter. She disconnected from us a long time ago. I have no idea where she is or what she's doing." Her hand rose and touched the plane of her chest just below her throat, sliding inside the open top of her shirt, as if she were feeling for a heartbeat. It was the same gesture that was in the photograph of her in the black halter.

"So you found the negative of me in that box. Were there any others?"

"Yes."

"What were they?"

"I'm not sure. I only glanced at them. Some men in army uniforms, a landscape. I don't think there were any others of you."

"What are you going to do with them?"

"I'll look at them this afternoon, make some prints, see what I have. Do you want copies?"

She held out the champagne flute and I filled it again. "What I would like," she said, "would be for you to put them in an ashtray and touch a match to them. Destroy them. Don't even look again at them." Her voice had lost its husky sexiness. It was flat and hard.

"Why?"

"You shouldn't ask why. Do what I suggest and your life will be a great deal easier. Go to Paris with Aaron's camera and take a photograph of a beautiful young woman."

"Someone like you?"

She turned to look at the photograph on the wall. "You could do worse."

"You're still a very attractive woman."

"*Attractive* woman. You could have chosen a better adjective."

"How about beautiful?"

"Too late, handsome." She withdrew her hand from her shirt, lifted the flute and drained it.

"Why should I burn those negatives?"

"First of all, you won't understand what they mean. Secondly, Aaron tucked them away where no one would find them, not even me. But you found them. An unfortunate accident. Trust me, dear boy, they're poisonous."

"You think I'll go home and melt those negatives down and not examine them more closely?"

"I think you might look at them and you might even make some prints, but you need to know that if you do, you're playing with fire and you could get badly burned." She set the flute on the floor next to her chair and stood. "Under other circumstances I might ask you to imagine that I'm still the woman in the photograph and spend the afternoon, but that's not going to happen, is it?"

"Apparently not."

"But if I were twenty years younger?"

"Like I said, you're still a beautiful woman."

"*Still.* There's another word that I don't like. Drink up," she said. She stood and went to the wall of glass. The egret sensed her movement and stretched its wings, lifting clumsily off the marsh.

"They look ungainly when they fly, but they have a delicate beauty when they stalk along the edge. And they're quite deadly. A single stab and some poor fish or a frog comes up, impaled on that beak. Beauty and death. Quite a combination." She turned to face me. Her hand had gone back to its place against her chest and I could swear that the tips of her fingers were touching her nipple.

"Remember what I said. I know about those negatives. So does Bill Fosberg. And by now, we don't know who else knows. Destroy them. Please. Or return them to me."

"I was wondering if you were going to ask for them back. You know what they are, don't you?"

"No. Aaron never told me what they were. Only that he had them and they were safely hidden and they should never get into anyone else's hands."

"Why is it that I have a hard time believing you?"

"The only thing you need to believe is that they are explosive. Like a time bomb that began ticking the moment you tipped them out of that box. And they won't give you much time."

"Who is *they*?"

"I don't know who they are. Only Aaron knew."

"And why don't I believe that, either?"

She didn't reply, only looked back through the glass at the egret. It had landed a few yards off and was moving slowly, lifting first one leg, then the other with meticulous care. The head was canted to one side so that an eye looked down at the edge of the water. I remembered that the word for birds like that was *stalkers*.

The afternoon was over. And she *was* quite beautiful. I drove back to the house, the image of her at the window looking out at the egret still with me. The first thing I did when I got home was go into the darkroom and get out the negatives. I set aside the one of Emma Sturgis and laid the others on the light table. There was an image of a person but the figure was clouded, as if it were enveloped in smoke. I put it in the enlarger and was startled by what came up. I sharpened the focus. It was grainier that Emma's photo and I gave it an extra f-stop. I slid the sheet of paper into the developer and, when the image began to appear, I could see why Emma Sturgis had warned me about the negatives.

It was not unlike Nick Ut's photograph of the terrified Vietnamese girl running naked from the chaos of a napalm raid on her village. She, too, had been terribly burned. But this photograph was different. It was a man, coming directly at the camera, and he was engulfed in flames. The only way I could tell it was a soldier was the helmet that capped the flames and the weapon he held in one hand. He wasn't running, He was simply a column of flame and black smoke and his face was not visible, and behind him were women and children and a few old men. They stood as if they were an audience witnessing some bizarre magic trick in which the magician lights himself on fire and strolls off.

Nick Ut's photo of the Vietnamese girl on fire running toward his camera won the Pulitzer Prize for him. It was the quintessential photo of that war, and Richard Nixon claimed it had been fixed; that it was a photo that had been doctored in order to drum up resistance to the war. But that photo was real, and so was the one I lifted from the developer tray and held under the light. I had never seen this photograph. It had never been published anywhere, that much I was sure of. This photograph, too, had to be Viet Nam. The faces of the people behind the burning figure were unmistakably Vietnamese. Aaron Sturgis had taken this photograph but it had remained out of sight for almost fifty years, the negative in the bottom of the Leica box. I moved the sheet to the stop bath, then to the fixer before I spread the other negatives on the light table and got out the loupe to look at them.

There were seven negatives: Emma in the black halter, the soldier on fire, and five others. One neg showed a soldier aiming his weapon at someone kneeling in front of him. It looked like a woman. She held an infant. Another negative showed the woman and the infant lying on the ground. The woman's head had been blown apart. So had the head of the infant.

There was a landscape that looked like a rice field or a flat meadow, but when I looked closely I could see that it was a photograph of a painting. There was a small plaque on the base of the frame, but I couldn't read the lettering. There was another negative with a helicopter in a clearing, dust whirling up and four men climbing into it. In the background, a village was in flames. The last negative was of five men standing in front of a metal hut. They were bare-chested, shirts off, two of them holding cans of beer.

Obviously something bad had happened. A soldier had gone up in flames. A woman and a child had been shot, probably by the soldier who stood with his gun over their bodies. His face was identifiable. He was one of the five soldiers in front of the metal hut. The village had been torched. What the painting of a field had to do with these was not clear. Nor was the reason that a photograph of Emma Sturgis would be included. Going back to Emma for an explanation would be useless. She had made it clear that I should not do what I was doing. I doubted that Bill Fosberg knew what they meant, and I wasn't sure I should make prints and show them to him. Emma had said he knew about the negatives, but I couldn't be sure that she meant he knew I had them or he knew what they meant. She had said that the negatives were *poisonous.* 'You're playing with fire,' were her words.

I put the negative of the burning soldier in the enlarger and made the first print. When I turned on the light, the photograph was horrific. Through the smoke and flames the soldier's open mouth could be seen. He must have been screaming. Everything about him was on fire except for the arm that held his weapon. It was canted out to one side. The smoke and flames billowed up under his helmet, curling around it to rise in a plume. The faces of the villagers in the background were impassive. They held no look of shock or horror—only the kind of intensity you might find on an audience at the circus watching the lion tamer put his head in the mouth of the lion. I pinned the print on the line to dry and put the next negative in the enlarger. This one had the dead woman and child in the foreground. It, too, was a horror. I wondered if the

Leica I had bought had been the camera that had taken these photographs.

Within the hour I had all seven prints. I laid them out and went over them carefully. The new print of Emma was not like the others. It had a museum portrait quality, fine-grained, evocative, and it was as good as anything I had ever seen. The war photos were grainier, stark, and contained no clues as to who the soldiers were or when the photos had been taken, although it appeared that they were Viet Nam war photos. There were no patches on their clothing, but the faces of the men were clear enough to be recognizable. The faces in the other photograph of the bare-chested young men in front of the metal hut were sharp. They were all young. They looked like teenagers. Only four men were climbing into the helicopter. Could the fifth man have been the one who had been on fire?

The photograph of the painting had been taken at some other time, like the one of Emma, since the negative was not part of the strip. I got out the loupe and looked at the plaque at the base of the photograph.

It was the title of the painting and the artist's name, followed by text:

Work from the scene of two murders, 1990
Marie Ruysell, born 1943

This painting is from a group of on-site works of the same location executed at the same time of day over a period of one year. Together they function as mug shots of the place where two murder victims were found, dragged from the Trinity River outside Ft. Worth, Texas.

There was no connection between Emma's portrait and this picture with the Viet Nam images. I put the photographs in an envelope along with the negatives and put them in my camera bag. Emma was right. I didn't have a clue as to what they meant, but it occurred to me that Aaron Sturgis had recorded a brutal act in Viet Nam and he had hidden the evidence of that act in the Leica box for fifty years.

I had an appointment to take some photos. The owner wanted me to set her up with her two dogs and take candids and with any luck I would sell her a glossy 8×10 and between the sitting fee and the photo I'd bring home two hundred bucks. It was not my favorite kind of a shoot, but stuff like this paid the rent.

The woman was a pushy old broad, fleshy-faced, a sour look, and her two dogs weren't prizes. One of them, Foxy, seemed more interested in goosing me with his sharp nose, and the other one, named Tallulah, kept dropping her ass on the ground and scooting around. "She's got a rash," the woman said, trying once again to corral the two of them.

She wanted to sit with the dogs next to the flower bed, but I wanted a plain background, something that would isolate the animals and the woman, give the photo a sense of contrast and maybe a bit of drama. I thought momentarily of Aaron Sturgis. He had never taken photographs of a crotchety old woman and her two out-of-control dogs. If he knew what I was doing with his camera, he would be whirling in his grave. Eventually we ended up next to the stucco back wall of her house and I got what I thought would be some decent shots. But I was pretty sure she wouldn't like them. What she wanted was to look sweet and the dogs to look cuddly, but that wasn't going to happen in this world. There would be at least one really good shot, that much I knew. And it would showcase her scowl and the scowling of the dogs and if she had a sense of humor, she would hang it over her fireplace; but she had no sense of humor. Several times she told me I was an unpleasant young man who obviously did not like dogs and I should try something else for a living.

"Foxy is a rescue dog, which is why he's so inquisitive, and Tallulah and I are both genetic descendants of Nefertiti."

I was glad when the hour ended.

When I got back to the house things had gone wrong. The front door was partly open, and when I looked inside, I was greeted by a shambles. Someone had been in the house and it had been torn to pieces. Chairs had their stuffing torn out, the ceiling fixtures had been pulled down, rugs piled against the wall. Every drawer in the kitchen had been emptied on the floor along with everything that had been in the cupboards. Someone had been looking for something and they hadn't left a stone unturned. The darkroom was a mess. Photographic paper was scattered on the floor, useless now that it had been exposed. My negative books were gone. Files that had contained photographs were emptied on the floor. And I knew what they had been looking for: the negatives that were in my camera bag.

"*Those negatives are poisonous*," Emma had said. I surveyed the damage. I hardly knew where to start.

It was midnight before the house returned to some semblance of order. Ruined chairs were in the garage, the rugs were back on the floor, although the ceiling fixtures still hung crazily askew. What pissed me off the most was the theft of my negative books. They wouldn't find the negs they were looking for and they would throw them away. Ten years of work had disappeared. Fortunately I had scanned some of the better stuff into my computer. That, too, had been fucked with, but it was obvious that they wanted the negatives and they hadn't found them. This wasn't over.

In the morning I telephoned Emma Sturgis. When she answered, I just said, "Who are they?"

"Who is this?" she asked.

"The handsome young man who brought champagne to your house. Somebody came to my house and broke in and searched it. They left it like a garbage dump. Obviously they were looking for those negatives"

There was a pause.

"I warned you."

"Whoever they are, they didn't exactly give me any time. Who are these people, Emma?"

"I don't know."

"You fucking *do* know. They've stolen ten years of my work and trashed my house and you know who they are."

"No," she said. "I don't. Aaron never told me who they were. Only that the negatives were important to them and that as long as he was alive they would never do anything."

"Well, they sure as hell did something yesterday afternoon! They came into my house and tore out the light fixtures, emptied every drawer and cabinet, and trashed my darkroom; and the only reason they didn't find those fucking negatives is because they were in my camera bag, sitting next to me while I photographed some old bitch and her two nasty dogs. Tell me, Emma. What do those negatives mean?"

"I don't know. All I know is that Aaron said that they were dangerous and that they were hidden away and I would never have to worry about them. Not as long as he was alive."

"The bastards stole my negative files. Ten years of work gone."

"I'm sorry."

"No, I don't think you're sorry. I think you know who these people are, and I think you can tell them to back off. I don't have a clue what those negatives mean, and I have no intention of showing them to anyone else and you can tell that to whoever is into the house-wrecking business."

"I don't know who they are, Michael."

"You don't know, or you won't tell me?"

"I don't know."

Her voice had lost its sexy undertone. I wanted to believe her.

"How do I get them to back off?" I said.

"Burn the negatives."

"And how will they know that the negatives are no longer in this world?"

"Let Bill Fosberg know what you have done."

"Fucking Bill Fosberg? That old son of a bitch is the conduit to these people, whoever they are?"

"Not on purpose. He told me about them which means if he didn't tell anyone else, then you and I are the only other people who know. So he told someone else. Who told someone. I don't know. I told *no* one. Believe me."

"So I go to Bill Fosberg and tell him I burned the negatives and whoever trashed my house will find out and they'll believe it? I don't think they'll believe it until they hold the negatives in their hands. Tell me who they are and they can have their fucking negatives."

"I told you. I don't know. Talk to Bill."

I hung up. And I remembered what she had said about the egret. Beauty and death. Quite a combination.

I decided that I didn't want to do this on the telephone. I went to Fosberg's shop. A pretty young woman was examining what looked like my Nikon SP. There were still a few classes at The Art Institute that required students to take photographs and work in their antiquated darkroom, just to get the feel of what it was like to shepherd a photograph from the subject to the print.

"I don't think I can afford that much," she was saying as I stepped next to her at the counter.

Bill looked at me, then at the girl. She must have been all of eighteen, sweet-faced, with long hair that was tied in a ponytail. Her sweatshirt was paint-spattered and she had a silver chain around her neck with what looked like coins from several countries hanging from it.

"You make your necklace?" I asked.

She looked at me. "Yes."

"I like it. Turning money into art. Nice touch."

She smiled.

"What are you asking for the Nikon, Bill?" I said. "Thirty-five bucks?"

"It's worth more than that, Michael," he said. He was scowling at me.

"That looks like the camera I traded in to you. What was it you gave me on the trade-in?"

The girl had stopped looking at the camera and was now looking intently at me.

"I've done some work on it, Michael," he said. Bullshit, I thought. The girl put the camera down on the counter. "I'll have to think about it," she said.

"I'll tell you what," Bill said. "I'm feeling particularly generous this morning. Call it fifty dollars and it's yours. And maybe Michael here, who's a fine professional photographer, will give you a lesson in how that camera works. How about it, Mike?"

The girl's face lit up.

"Make sure he gives you a half a dozen rolls of Ilford Pro film," I said.

"Mikey, do you know what that costs?" Bill said.

"I should," I said. "And that would make the price for that camera just about right."

The girl looked at Bill. "Could I have some film?" she asked tentatively. Bill put four rolls of Ilford on the counter and watched as she counted out five ten-dollar bills.

"You'll give me a lesson?" she asked.

"Not right now," I said. "Give me your number and I'll give you a call." I took a business card out of my pocket. "Better yet, you call me and we'll work out something. It shouldn't take more than half an hour."

She took my card, thanked Bill, and left the shop, carrying the Nikon. It was silent for a moment, and then Bill said, "You prick. You think I can stay in business by giving things away?"

"You gave me twenty bucks off a camera for that SP and a Minolta that's in perfect shape. You keystone it for forty bucks and you're way ahead. Ten bucks worth of film won't break your ass."

"My, oh my," Bill said. "Who stuck a stick up your ass this morning?"

"It was yesterday afternoon. Somebody came to my house, searched it from top to bottom, trashed the whole fucking house, ripped apart my darkroom, stole ten years worth of negatives, and flashed several hundred dollars worth of paper. And you may be the person responsible."

"What the hell are you talking about?"

"Yesterday I saw Emma Sturgis. You told her about those negatives."

"Why not? They belonged to her husband."

"She told me to burn them. Or give them back to her."

Bill was silent.

"And when I got home my house looked like a cyclone had hit it. The roof was still on, but that was about all."

"And what makes you think I had anything to do with it?"

"Because I told you about those negatives and you told Emma and within hours somebody was looking for them."

"How do you know that's what they were looking for?"

"Emma said they were a threat to my well-being. And apparently you told somebody else."

"What makes you think Emma didn't tell someone. She have you occupied while they were trashing your house?"

"No. It happened while I was photographing an old bitch and her two crazy dogs. And I'm not sure I know what to think. I don't have a fucking clue why those negatives are so important. There's the one of Emma, one of a painting of a field in Texas, and five others that were taken in Viet Nam. Two of them are fucking explosive, bad stuff happening, but there's no way to tell who the people are. Who did you tell about the negatives?"

"Jesus, I don't know. There was a guy in yesterday looking for Aaron's cameras. He said he knew Aaron and heard I had them and he bought the 4x5 and the Rollei TLR for nine grand. Didn't bat an eyelash. He wanted to know if there were any boxes or manuals and I gave him everything Emma gave me. He asked if I had any old negatives that Aaron had left behind. I may have mentioned the Leica and those negatives. How the hell was I supposed to know what they were. You fucking didn't tell me!"

"You know the name of this guy?"

"He paid cash."

"How would he know you had Aaron's cameras?"

"The only person who would have known was Emma."

"So maybe Emma knows who this guy is. Somebody wants those negatives badly. And I want to give them to that somebody since I have no use for them and don't know what the hell they mean. And why would he be so anxious to buy the cameras?"

"You found the negatives in the Leica box. Maybe he thinks there are some in the camera bodies. Or in old manuals. Maybe he just wanted to pump me for information about those negatives. How the hell would I know? Two days ago I didn't even know those negatives existed!"

"If this guy comes back in, you tell him I have his goddamn negatives and he can have them if he'll get off my back."

"Tell me again what they are."

"There's the one of Emma. I gave you a print. There's one of a painting of a river in Texas. Not a photographic landscape, a photo of a painting in a museum. There's one of a soldier who got set on fire, and one of a woman and a child and a soldier with a gun, and another of that soldier. But the woman and the kid are lying on the ground at his feet and they have their heads blown off. There's another one of five guys standing in front of a hut, probably their quarters; and one of four guys getting into a helicopter. That's it, Bill. You can't tell who these guys are, although the one of the group of them in front of the hut is in focus, and if you knew what somebody looked like forty years ago, you could identify him. But there aren't any names or signs or insignia patches."

"So somebody did a bad thing forty years ago and Aaron kept the negatives. Maybe that somebody wants them back."

"Jeez, Bill, it was fucking forty years ago. They were all teenage soldiers. Who's gonna care?"

"Somebody cares. Enough to trash your house. And pay nine grand for some cameras that were worth seven. I should have asked ten." He paused. "Maybe you should just give them to Emma."

"I'm not sure I trust her, Bill. She may be lying about not knowing who wants them. And I think the fact that I know what's on them is making somebody very nervous. I have the feeling that I'm out of my league on this."

"Then give them to me."

I looked at him. Ninety years old, and sly as a fox.

"No," I said. "I'm not sure I trust you, either."

I tried calling Emma when I got back to the house but there was no answer. Then I remembered Ray, who lived down the block, a Viet Nam vet who was a retired electrician. I took the manila envelope and walked down the street. Ray was in the back yard cleaning up his BBQ. Powerfully built, close-cropped grey hair, he looked younger than his sixty years.

"Hey, Mike," he said when he saw me. "What's up?"

"Do me a favor, Ray?" I asked.

"Depends on the favor," he replied.

"I've got some pictures I came across and I was hoping you could help me. Some of them were taken in Viet Nam."

He wiped his hands on a towel, laid the towel across the grill, and said, "Come on in the kitchen. Evelyn's out shopping. I'll buy you a beer."

The kitchen was squeaky clean—tile shining, counters empty. Both Evelyn and Ray had a thing for neatness. He took two beers out of the refrigerator, opened them, set a coaster under each bottle on the table.

"Let's see what you have," he said.

I laid the manila envelope on the table and took out the photo of the five guys in front of the hut.

"Half a squad," he said. "A squad consists of two fire teams of five soldiers each. In Nam we tended to split them, one group of five entering a village, the other holding back, covering their ass. Each team had a sergeant in command."

I showed him the photo of the four men climbing into the helicopter.

"Bugging out," he said. "Either they lost one guy or he's on another chopper. Jesus, that brings back bad memories. I can hear the fucking chopper blades and smell that smoke. Maybe napalm. Could be that air cover torched the village."

"Napalm?" I asked.

"Comes in a powder. They mix it with aviation fuel and some kind of gel so it sticks to whatever it hits. Fucking deadly stuff. You ever see that photograph of that kid running at the camera burning? That was napalm. You don't forget that smell. I used to wake up smelling that shit years after it was over."

"What about these?" I asked. I slid the photo of the burning soldier onto the table.

He looked away. Then looked back. "Fucking trap," he said. "They booby-trapped everything. I know that one. You went into a hooch and a pot filled with gas tipped over and suddenly you were drenched in it and somebody threw a match at you. I saw that happen more than once." He slid the picture under the envelope.

"And this?" I added. I pointed to the woman kneeling in front of the soldier and then the one of her and the child dead on the ground.

"Retribution."

"She was the one who lit the soldier on fire?"

"Who knows? Who the fuck cares? Somebody goes into a hooch and comes out on fire and you want to kill someone. Make a statement."

"So she might not have been the one who threw the match?"

"My guess is nobody knew who threw the match. Where did you get these pictures?"

"Negatives from a guy who was a photographer in Viet Nam. He's dead. I found them in an old box."

"It's fucking water under the bridge, Mike. Those guys, whoever they are, are sixty years old now. They all had their nightmares. Some of them are dead. Do yourself a favor and take these fucking things and burn them."

"Somebody already told me to do that."

"Christ," he said. "I look at those and it's like fucking yesterday. They're just pictures to you but I can smell them. I can smell that guy cooking and smell the napalm and smell the shit they used in the rice paddies and there were birds. Jesus, there were birds like you've never seen, gorgeous things, like jewels in the jungle, and they used to shriek, scare the shit out of you, and I can hear the chopper. And hear that poor fucker screaming. It's like I'm swimming in a lake and the water is filthy and I'm drowning in it, can't get my breath, and no matter how hard I swim, the shore never gets any closer."

"I'm sorry. I shouldn't have asked you to look at them."

"It doesn't matter, Mike. You weren't even born when they were taken. And I'm sure some guy is taking pictures like that in Iraq or Afghanistan right now."

"Is there any way to find out who those guys were? What outfit they were with?"

"Not from these. Could be anywhere."

"Can I buy you a drink?" I asked.

"No. Right now that would be a bad idea. I'll take a rain check, though." He slid the pictures together in a stack and turned them over. "Burn the fuckers, Mike," he said.

Whatever else happened, I needed to pay my bills. I had bought a pack of paper from Bill and I needed to do a proof sheet of the woman and her dogs. It was possible that I had something she would buy. Once people paid the sitting fee of sixty bucks, they bought at least one print. I would worry about Aaron Sturgis' negatives later.

It felt good to be back in the darkroom. I mixed new chemicals, developed the film from the shoot, and when the negative strip was dry, I laid the negs on the light table. There was one print of the old bitch and the two dogs she would like. It was sentimental, with the woman surrounded by flowers, holding the two dogs in an armlock, and it was the closest thing to making the trio look like you'd want them for neighbors. And the one I liked, against the stark stucco wall, her face in shadow and the two dogs showing their teeth in manic grins, was the one that was the winner.

"You're fucking good at times, Michael," I said out loud. The little Leica had a gem of a lens. The grain was fine and the woman's sour smile was a sharp shadow across the fleshy folds of her face, and I thought, this photograph would hang next to anybody's photograph in any gallery anywhere, and I felt satisfied.

I tried calling Emma again. Still no answer. I drove to her house, but there was no one home. I even went around behind the house, wading in the marsh grass so I could look in the wall of glass. Nobody there. The egret was gone, too.

Back at the house I looked again at the photographs. Ray had said there was no way to identify anyone from the Viet Nam photos. The only other photo was the one of the painting. That's when I called Chuck Harrington. He's the curator of the photo archives at the Museum of Modern Art. I asked him how I would go about tracking down the artist of a painting.

"Not my department, Mike. What have you got?"

"I've got a photograph of a painting and I'm hoping that I can find out something about it. Or the artist."

"What kind of a painting?"

"It's an oil, done in 1990 by an artist named Marie Ruysell.

"Is she American?"

"I think so. The painting is of a scene in Texas."

"Nancy Sonoma. She's the one to call. Modern American paintings. She's not with the museum. She works for Sotheby's in The City."

He gave me her number.

Nancy Sonoma took only a few moments to find the artist. "She lives in Fort Worth, Texas. Her paintings hang in a number of museums. The painting you describe is in the Brooklyn Museum's collection of modern American art."

"Can you tell me where she lives? How I can get in touch with her?"

"That I can't do. But she has an agent who might be able to help." She gave me the agent's number.

The agent wanted to know if I was a collector.

"No," I said. "I'm a professional photographer and I'm working on a series of photographs of artists. I'm hoping that Ms. Ruysell would be willing to be a part of the series."

"How did you happen to select her?"

"One of her paintings. It hangs in the Brooklyn Museum and it's titled, *Work from the Scene of Two Murders.*"

"Of course," she said. "There was a series of paintings done at that location. If you give me your number, I'll let Marie know about your project. If she's interested, she can call you."

"I'm working under a rather tight time frame," I said. "It would help if she could say yes or no as soon as possible." I detected a note of impatience in the woman's voice.

"I'll let her know," she said.

I had one other card I could play. I called Graham Lukas, the police chief in Fairfax. My town is only 7500 people, tucked into the hills of Marin County north of San Francisco. The police department consists of a woman who drives around in an electric scooter marking tires, eight officers, a sergeant, and a chief. The chief is a guy I went to high school with. In high school he would have been listed as 'least likely to become a police chief' and 'most likely to get arrested,' but Graham had gone off to college, got a degree in criminal justice, took a job as a patrolman in Oakland, then moved up to sergeant in Fairfax, and now he was the chief. Stocky, a shiny bald head, he looked older than his thirty-five years. It seemed like he knew everyone in town, and when he stopped in at The Koffee Klatch for his mid-morning coffee, he was met with smiles and backslapping.

I asked him if I could buy him a cup of coffee.

"What's up?" he asked.

"I've got a question maybe you can answer."

"You got some problems?"

"Maybe."

So I met him at the cafe on the corner a block from the city hall. I slid the photo of the painting across the table.

"What's this?" he asked.

"It's a photo of a painting. It says that it's the scene of two murder victims that got dragged from a river. It was done in 1990. Is there any way I can find out anything about those two murders?"

Graham raised his eyebrows. "This isn't just idle curiosity, is it?" He sipped at his coffee. He wore Levis, a dark blue shirt with his chief's badge on the pocket, and there was a small radio clipped to his belt. No weapon, no cop's uniform, no handcuffs or nightstick. If it weren't for the badge, he could have been mistaken for a contractor or a plumber.

"Somebody searched my house. Turned everything upside down. I came into possession of some photographic negatives and they're apparently something that somebody wants badly, and I'd like to give them to that somebody; but I don't know who it is."

"Somebody broke into your house?"

"Yes. Two days ago."

"And you didn't file a report with us?"

"I guess that's what I'm doing now."

"These photographs. What are they?"

"Some old Viet Nam pictures. I checked them out with Ray Sanchez and he says it's old stuff. You can't even tell what outfit the guys were in."

"So what's this stuff about some painting?"

"This photo is of that painting. And I think the murders that are referred to by the artist are connected to the negatives. So I'd like to find out what that was all about."

"Mike, are you playing some kind of Sherlock Holmes? You leave that crap to people like us. File the breaking-and-entering report, give me the negatives, and I'll lock them up for you."

"All I'm asking is for you to help me figure out that painting."

He sighed, finished his coffee and set the cup on the table. "Promise me that you'll file a report and bring those negatives in. I'll find out what I can. When and where were these murders committed?"

"Fort Worth Texas. 1990. They pulled two bodies from the Trinity River. That's all I know."

"It should be enough. And get some decent locks on your house."

On the way home I drove to Emma's place but there was no sign of her. I went by Bill Fosberg's shop but it was closed. That wasn't unusual. Bill kept odd hours. Sometimes the shop was closed for several days in a row.

Back at the house I printed up proofs of the woman and dog photos and got them ready to mail. I spent an hour re-wiring the ceiling fixture in the kitchen where it had been pulled down. The house was beginning to look normal again. On the front and back doors, I installed the deadbolts I had bought at the hardware store on the way home. They looked like overkill. I knew that if somebody wanted to get into the house all they would have to do would be to break a window. Still, Graham had said to put in new locks and I had done what he asked. It was late afternoon when I poured myself a scotch and went out onto the little back patio . From there I can see Mt. Tamalpais, a dusty green in the summer light. The sun was beginning to go off the mountain and the folds were turning dark. If I squinted my eyes, I could imagine I was in the Sierra Nevada mountains. I finished the scotch, made another one, and was sitting down when the phone rang.

It was Graham.

"Two homeless guys," he said. "Both got their heads bashed in and dumped in the river. One was a John Doe; the other was a Chip Piper, homeless Viet Nam veteran. Next of kin is a Cindy Piper in Benbow, Texas. Not far from Forth Worth. That's it. VA buried him in a military cemetery in Dallas. When you gonna bring those negatives in?"

"Tomorrow. Right now I'm having a scotch and looking at the mountain."

"Not a bad idea."

"Thanks, Graham."

"Not a problem," he said. "But don't do any wild-hair-up-your-ass kind of thing and go off half-cocked. Did you get some locks?"

"Yeah. Two fucking big deadbolts that look like they belong on the San Quentin prison gates."

"It'll slow them down. Be a good boy and bring those negatives in."

That night he showed up. Actually, it was almost three o'clock in the morning, and I was half-asleep, when I was heard someone pounding at my door. I got up and I flipped on the outside light and the knocking stopped. Through the peephole in the door I could see him, a stocky man, Hispanic, built like a tank—wide shoulders, square body. He wore a Harcartt coat and gloves and he stood away from the door, his hands in front of him. He didn't say anything, just stood there, his hands crossed in front of his body, and it occurred to me that he was putting his hands where I could see them. It was a sign of somebody who was familiar with being questioned by cops. Somewhere I had read that if you ever get pulled over, you should put your hands on the steering wheel, cross them in front of you where they can be seen, make sure the cop can see that you don't have a weapon.

"What can I do for you?" I yelled through the door.

"You Michael McSwain?"

"Yes."

"I've got a message for you."

"At this hour? What's the message?"

"It's fucking cold out here."

"Is that the message?"

He held up his hands, said, "I just want to give you the message. It's easier if I'm inside. I don't like talking out here."

"I don't know who the hell you are, buddy, and there's no way I'm letting you inside."

"Fucking cold out here," he said.

"You already told me that," I said.

He was Mexican or Central American, his brown face shiny in the light from the bulb over the door. He might have been one of those guys who stands on the corner in East San Rafael at dawn, waiting for a contractor to pick him up for day work, but somehow he was different. He didn't have that day-laborer look. He crossed his hands in front again.

"So," I said, "what's the message?"

"You have something that does not belong to you."

"You lose something?"

"No. You have some photographic negatives and they belong to another man. He would like them back."

"They belonged to a man who is dead. I bought them."

"If you give them to me, your troubles will be over."

"I don't know who the fuck you are."

"If you do not want to give them to me, then you will be visited by other people. They will not be so polite."

"Who sent you?"

"I don't know. I'm just the messenger."

"Is this a threat? Are you saying that if I don't give you those negatives, I might get hurt?"

"Like I said, I'm just the messenger."

"Who sent you?"

His face was impassive.

"Who the fuck sent you?"

He smiled. "Nobody sent me. I'm a messenger from God."

"Funny," I said, "you don't look like an angel. What does God look like?"

"I do not know. Maybe he looks like you. Maybe he looks like me."

"What's that supposed to mean?"

"If you keep those negatives, you will regret it. That's what God said to tell you."

As he stepped away from the door, he half-turned, keeping an eye on the door as he stepped into the darkness. I had the feeling that the messenger from God wasn't somebody to tangle with.

I began to shake. I went back to the bedroom and looked in my camera bag. The manila envelope with the prints and the negatives was still there. I went back into the living room and looked at the dead bolt on the front door. I wished I had a gun. But of course I didn't. I've never owned a gun in my life. I thought about calling the cops, but what could they do? All I had was a guy who knocked on my door at three o'clock in the morning and asked for some negatives. And he said others would not be so polite. Nobody had actually threatened me.

I wrapped myself in a blanket, turned on the TV, and watched an old movie, finally dozing off, only to wake when I heard the garbage truck out front. I heard the grinding of the compactor and then the hiss as the air brakes went off, and the laboring motor as it climbed the hill.

I got dressed and made some coffee and tried to figure out what to do. If I took the negatives to Graham and he locked them in the police safe, my trouble would not be over, since I would be the only one who could get them out and whoever had sent the angel from God would not rest until he had them. I was pretty sure Emma knew who he was. Or perhaps Bill Fosberg.

It occurred to me that Cindy Piper might be the key. She was next of kin to the Viet Nam veteran who had been pulled dead from that river. And that scene was in the photograph of the painting. By photographing that painting, Sturgis had connected the murder of two men, one of them a Viet Nam vet, to the other photographs. There had to be a connection. Perhaps she knew some of the men in the photograph of the five soldiers. I called directory assistance, but there was no Cindy Piper listed in Benbow, Texas. I went on my computer and tried Googling her. Nothing came up. I tried Benbow, Texas, and got the number of a Sheriff's substation in town. I called the number and told the officer who answered that I was trying to track down a relative of a dead Viet Nam soldier. His name was Chip Piper and the information I had was that he had a relative who lived in Benbow.

"Who are you?" the voice asked.

"I work for a veteran's organization and we have some citations that surfaced on his records and we'd like to give them to her, if she still exists."

"So what is it that you want?"

My breath stopped. I had caught the brass ring. The Cindy Piper I wanted was there!

"Just an address."

There was a pause. I thought, now he's thinking this is some kind of a scam, and he's not about to give me an address even if he has one.

"Look," I said. "Why don't I give you my number and you can call back. That way you'll know I'm on the level. All we want to do is mail something to her. She doesn't have to do anything, doesn't have to contact anybody."

"Where are you calling from?"

"California."

"How are you going to know the Cindy Piper who lives here is the one you want?"

"I've got the service records that show her as next of kin. He was found dead in the Trinity River in 1990. At least that's what the burial records and the death certificate show."

Another pause. Apparently that was enough. "Yeah, we got a Cindy Piper. Her brother is the dead guy you're talking about. Her old man, the one she lives with, isn't exactly unknown to us. You might say he's a regular customer."

"Can I get an address?"

"All you'll get is Arroyo Seco Road. You send your letter to the postmaster in Benbow and he'll get it out there."

"Can I get a telephone number?"

"About all you could get would be the Jiffy store about a mile from where she lives. You want to talk to her, you'll have to come to Benbow."

I thanked him and hung up. I had an address, there was no telephone, and it sounded like wherever it was that she lived, there was little chance that I could talk to her unless I actually stood on her doorstep. And I needed her to look at that photo-graph and perhaps identify the men in it.

So I decided to do what Graham Lukas had warned me not to do. I would get in my old Toyota and drive to Texas, and I would show her the photograph. It would get me away from my house and put me out of the reach of whoever had sent the angel of God. I Googled the directions to Benbow, Texas. Three long days. A day to Los Angeles, and then another two days east to Fort Worth. I would be gone six days, Nobody would know where I was. And if I found out nothing from Cindy Piper, then I could come back and wait for another mes-senger. Or go to Graham and ask for his help.

I went to the bank and drew out five hundred dollars, which pretty much emptied my account. I gassed up the car and drove across the Richmond Bridge to the East Bay, then south toward I-5. It was already ten o'clock. I would not arrive in L.A. until after dark.

Traffic on the Interstate down the Central Valley moved at nearly eighty miles an hour, but I kept under that, afraid my Toyota wouldn't be up to it. At one point I drafted behind a Walmart sixteen-wheeler for nearly an hour, letting him suck me along, saving gas. The flat fields stretched out on both sides, mostly the dull suede brown of summer, occasionally a green that was irrigated. The Coast Range was blue along the right side of the valley, and far to the left was the dim gray outline of the Sierras. It was late afternoon when I climbed the Grapevine and dropped down into the Los Angeles basin. The smog was dirty brown and the traffic was fierce, and it was another two hours before I climbed out of the basin on the San Bernardino side. Car lights were on, the mountains on either side were dark, but I wanted to keep on going. I stopped to get gas, had a greasy burger and fries at a Sam's drive-through, and pushed on.

It was ten o'clock when I stopped at a motel just over the Arizona line in a small town named Parker. The vacancy sign was still lit and it was obvious why. A low line of rooms faced a rough parking lot, chunks of asphalt missing. The sign on the street was fixed to a post next to the telephone pole and said **SENECA MOTEL,** and under it **HBO Kitchenettes QUIET.** The paint was faded. The office had a sheet of paper tacked to the door that read Ring Bell for Service, but when I pushed the bell nothing happened. I opened the door and inside was a counter and behind it a half door and beyond that the living room with a large TV flickering with cartoons. A dog came rushing at the half door, barking furiously, a brown pit bull, its flat head lunging at me. It was joined by another black-and-white pit bull and then a child, a toddler no taller than the head of the second dog. The dogs swirled around the child, charging against the door and barking, and I waited, half expecting one of the dogs to clamp its jaw onto the child. A large woman appeared, opened the half-door, and held the dogs back, closing it behind her.

"You need something?" she asked.

"A room."

She pushed a registration card at me.

"Fill this out. Thirty-one a night plus tax."

She gave me the key to room eleven with an orange plastic badge attached, and a TV control device. The cracked back was held on with duct tape.

Room eleven was almost at the end of the row of doors. The parking lot was broad, asphalt with patches and raw spots, and each door was fronted by a tiny concrete stoop not more than three feet wide. When I opened the door I was met with a stale smell that was faintly reminiscent of something that had died. Perhaps a rat in a wall or something in the kitchenette.

The room was small with a double bed covered with a brown and orange bedspread, the colors swirled in a muddy pattern, and my first instinct was to dump it on the floor at the side of the bed. Under it was a brown electric blanket, the cords in the blanket like ropes.

The bathroom was paneled in plastic sheets of fake tile, the yellow of overdone eggs, and the shower was tiny, a tiled compartment. Cracked linoleum covered the floor and the towels were small and threadbare, but clean.

The bedroom was paneled in plywood with a shiny finish, almost plastic in the light of the single overhead bulb. I turned off the light and the mahogany-colored walls became dark. I opened the window to let in air, sat on the end of the bed. Through the window I could see a dog-run, partially covered by a blue tarp on the far side of the asphalt, a single floodlight still on. A chain-link fence separated the dog-run from the parking lot. A dog yapped somewhere behind the tarp.

It was after midnight, I was exhausted, and I was six hundred miles from my house and Emma Sturgis and Bill Fosberg and whoever wanted the negatives. Tomorrow I would be even farther. I could hear Graham Lukas saying, "You're a fucking idiot, McSwain." I fell asleep with my clothes on.

The next morning I was on the road before it was light. I had breakfast in an all-night diner and drove, only stopping for gas and some candy bars, reaching Texas by early evening. The map showed I still had ten hours to go.

Another cheap motel in a town named Corridas and I was on the last leg at four in the morning, driving through endless miles of sagebrush and flatness, and I wondered about the lives of people who called this home.

Fort Worth came up in the late afternoon. I found the town of Benbow on the map and the two-lane highway that circled north of the city. I was tired now, and I concentrated on the road, gripping the wheel so hard my knuckles were white.

I remembered something Rico, the kid who mowed my lawn, used to say. *"Camaron que se dureme, so lo llena la corriente."* When the shrimp falls asleep, then the current carries him away. It was an expression his father had used. Usually he rapped Rico hard on top of his head with a calloused knuckle when he said it. "If you don't pay attention, you'll fuck up." Rico had memorized it, and I was surprised to realize that I had memorized it, too.

It was just after four o'clock when I swung off the Interstate along old Highway 66 twenty miles beyond Fort Worth. I drove all the way through Benbow, past the Dairy Queen, past the grocery store to the far edge of town, then reversed myself. I had gone no more than ten blocks. I came back, looking for street signs, but there were none. I stopped at the single gas station and asked the attendant, a lanky man wearing a greasy baseball cap, where I could find Arroyo Seco.

"Who you looking for?" he asked.

"Cindy Piper."

He pointed down the street. "You go to the stop sign. Then you turn left and go until the pavement ends. Keep on going maybe a quarter of a mile. You can't miss it. They got lots of dogs."

I followed his directions. The pavement ended and the gravel road went straight out into sagebrush-covered flatland. I went a quarter of a mile, and off to the left there was a narrow dirt track littered with broken glass and scraps of tattered plastic clinging to the scraggly sagebrush. I could see a house, a peeling ten-wide trailer on cement blocks. It stood in a square compound outlined by sagging cyclone fencing, and the ground was bare, scrubbed of all vegetation by dogs and cars.

There was an air of abandonment about the place: an old refrigerator tipped on its face along with worn-out tires, bottles, a sofa with no cushions that had faded in the desert sun until the fabric had rotted, a battered three-wheel ATV, cans, cloudy plastic bottles, and sun-dried piles of dog shit. Three dogs appeared, barking and dashing back and forth along the fence. They were as scruffy as the building, continuously tumbling together in their excitement, snapping at each other as they did so. They appeared so suddenly that I momentarily wondered where they had come from, but I realized they must stay under the trailer where it would be cooler, out of the merciless sun. There was a gate in the fence secured by a piece of twisted wire, and I stopped the car in front of it and got out. By now the dogs were rushing at the gate, up on their hind legs, snarling and barking, falling back on each other in a tangle of dusty fur.

"Hey!" I shouted. "Anybody here?" If there was anybody there, I thought, they would have heard the dogs by now. I called out again, "Anybody home?"

I was watching the doorway of the trailer when I became aware that someone was standing at the corner of the building, watching me. It was a man with lank hair wearing only a pair of gray boxer shorts, holding a pistol in one hand.

I put my hands over my head and shouted, "Take it easy, I don't want anything!" I took several steps back from the gate.

The man shouted at the dogs, "Shut the hell up," and bending over, picked up an empty beer bottle at his feet, hurling it at the dogs. It hit one of them with a thump, the dog's bark turned to a shrill whine and, tucking its tail in a curl between its legs, it made a beeline for a hiding place, disappearing into the trash at the skirt of the house. The other two dogs followed.

The man said nothing more, stepping out of the narrow band of shade offered by the side of the house.

"I don't want anything," I repeated, resting my hands on top of my head. I could feel the sweat suddenly cooling under my upraised arms.

The man spoke. "You don't want nothing, how come you're standing at my fence?" He absently scratched the inside of his thigh with the barrel of the pistol.

"I just want to ask something," I said. "That's all."

"Then you do want something." The voice came slowly, as if the man were not fully conscious or, worse yet, I thought, he might be stoned.

"All I want is some information."

The man said nothing.

"I just want to know if Cindy Piper lives here."

"Why would you want to know that?"

"I'm trying to find out something about the death of her brother."

"You the police?"

"No. I'm a photographer from California and I have some pictures that were taken in Viet Nam, and I think one of the men in one of the pictures is her brother."

"What's that got to do with her?" The reply was laconic and I realized the slow-voiced man was fully in control

"I'm hoping she can identify her brother and maybe some of the other men."

"Why would she want to do that?"

"It's a long story. Somebody wants those pictures bad enough to do me some harm and I'm trying to find out who they are."

"Why would Cindy give a fuck about what happens to you? She don't know you from Adam."

"All I want her to do is look at a photograph. Is that too much to ask?"

"What's in it for her?" The dogs had crept out from under the house and were grouped around his legs. Another good photograph, I thought. This one could go next to the one of the woman and her two dogs. But I knew this was a man who was not about to let me take his photograph.

"I could pay her for her time."

"How much?"

"Twenty dollars?"

"Piss off," he said.

"All she has to do is look at a photograph. It takes a few seconds."

"My guess is it's worth more than twenty bucks to you. Otherwise you would not of come all the way from California to ask her to look at your picture." He raised the pistol so that it pointed directly at me and silently mouthed what looked like the word *POW*. Behind him the flat plain wavered in the heat. Everything seemed blue in that instant, the hard blue of the sky, the soft shimmering blue of the distant line of mountain peaks. Even the expanse of sagebrush that stretched away in all directions had taken on a blue cast.

"You got two choices," the man said. "You can give me a hunderd bucks and I tell you where Cindy is and maybe she looks at your picture and you get the fuck out of here, or you take your picture and get the fuck out of here. I don't give a shit."

I fished my wallet out of my back pocket, drew out five twenties and held them up.

"How much more you got in there?" he asked.

"Enough to get back to California."

Boxer Shorts came out toward the gate. He was wearing huaraches, hand-made from pieces of old tire casings, and they flopped on his feet as he approached the wire. He held out his hand. In the bright sunlight I could see that his face was pock-marked with acne and his feet were dark brown, blackened in places, as if he had not bathed in some time. I pushed the bills through the wire. He took them, folding them inside his fist and walked back to the door of the trailer. He rapped on the door with the barrel of the pistol.

"Cindy!" he called out. "Come on out here. Your good-looking boyfriend from California showed up and he wants to show you his dick."

The door opened and a woman stood there. She was in her sixties and she wore a shapeless dress, but her hair was bright orange and it was swept up on top of her head in a flaming crown.

"What's this all about?" she asked.

Boxer Shorts waved the pistol in my direction. "That fella wants you to look at a picture. Says it's a picture of Chip when he was in Viet Nam."

She stepped down into the sun, shading her eyes with one hand. She came across the dirt to the gate. Unlike the man she was neat and clean, and I could see that the nails on the hand shading her eyes were neatly manicured.

"Who are you?" she asked.

"Michael McSwain. I'm from California and I'm trying to find out if Chip Piper was your brother."

"And if he was?"

"I have a photograph here." I took the picture of the five men out of the manila envelope and held it up to the wire. "Is one of those men your brother?"

She stepped close to the wire, still shading her eyes with her hand.

"That's Chip," she said. "Next to the end. Where did you get that picture?"

"It was left to me by a photographer who's dead. He took it in Viet Nam. Do you know the names of any of the other men?"

"The one next to Chip on the end, that was Ronnie Milsap. Him and Chip joined up together. He got killed the year after Chip did."

"He was the other man who was dragged out of the Trinity River?"

"How come you know about that?"

"Somebody wants this picture and some others. They want them bad enough to do me great harm. Maybe kill me. But I don't know who they are. Do you know what outfit your brother was in?"

"Fourth Infantry They called it the Iron Horse. Him and Ronnie trained at Fort Carson, Colorado.

"Do you know when this photograph would have been taken?"

"They was in Viet Nam in 1966 or '67."

"Is there anybody else in that photograph that you recognize?"

"There's his sergeant. Big guy on the other end. I don't know his name. Chip just called him Sarge. And one of the other guys would be Luther. The shorter one. Don't remember his last name. I don't know who the other guy is. Why does somebody want your photographs so bad?"

"It's a long story."

"Time's up!" Boxer Shorts called out. "You want anything else, pony up again."

Cindy turned to Boxer Shorts. "What do you mean, 'pony up'? He paid you to talk to me?"

"That's my business." He waved the pistol in my direction.

"Thank you, ma'm," I said.

"You think whoever wants your photographs had something to do with Chip's death?"

"I don't know."

"Somebody beat his head in and dumped him in the river and the Fort Worth cops just said another homeless drunk, and they didn't do nothing. Same with Ronnie."

"The Forth Worth police listed Ronnie as a John Doe."

"I told them who he was, but they wasn't interested. Once they found out he was a homeless drunk, it didn't matter much to them anymore."

"They listed your brother's name and where he came from and that he was a veteran. He got buried by the VA in Dallas."

"They wouldn't of done that if I hadn't put up a fuss."

Boxer Shorts was now standing next to her. "Time's up," he repeated. "Clear on out of here."

I reached in my pocket, pulled out a business card and pushed it through the fence toward her.

"Can I have that picture?" she asked.

I rolled it into a tube and put it through the chain link fence. She took it, unrolled it, and looked at it again. "Thank you," she said.

"If you remember anything else, please call me," I said and turned toward the car.

"You find out anything, you let me know," Cindy called out.

Boxer Shorts had his hand on her shoulder and was steering her back toward the door of the trailer. The dogs had resumed their barking at the gate. And I knew which three of the five men were dead and what the first name of one of the others was. It was more than I knew when I set out from home.

10

I found a motel and crashed, and I slept until ten o'clock the
following morning. I found a cafe and had a breakfast of bacon and eggs and biscuits and gravy and a side order of sausage
and more buttermilk biscuits and coffee. It was half the price it
would have been in a café at home.

I thought about what Cindy Piper had said. Chip and
Ronnie had trained at Fort Collins, Colorado. It was between
me and California, and there was the chance that I could find
out who the third and fourth men were. If I could isolate the
squad, then I could get a last name for Luther. And I would
be one step closer to finding out who wanted the negatives. It
was a long shot but I was in no hurry to get home. The messenger from God might be waiting for me with some of his
friends. And I was bothered by the fact that two of the men
in that squad had been murdered and dumped in the Trinity
River. Had they, in a drunken moment, told someone what
they had seen in Viet Nam? Was the soldier who had killed the
woman and the child the person who wanted those negatives?
The village had gone up in flames. Who had ordered that? The

sergeant? Or was he the one who had been set on fire? And why was the image of Emma Sturgis kept with the other negatives? The murder of two soldiers from the same squad was too co-incidental and the photograph of the painting that had led me to them was no accident. Aaron Sturgis had put that negative there for a reason.

Fort Collins was twelve hours away, and I drove until I entered Colorado. It was dark and I looked for another cheap motel. I only had a hundred and fifty dollars left and most of that would be consumed by gas. The motel I found was twenty-five dollars a night. There was a reason. I paid in cash and went to the room. It was dingy and smelled musty, but there was a bed and I dropped my bag on it, stripped, and went into the tiny bathroom. When I turned on the light there was a scurry of black things. A rush of cockroaches crossed the floor and I involuntarily drew back. Shit, I thought, it's the original roach motel. I turned the hot water on and washed as many of them off the wall of the shower as I could, watching the puddle of wriggling black go down the drain. I showered, soaping my-self, luxuriating in the hot water, and when I stepped out, more cockroaches were scurrying across the cracked linoleum floor. I dried myself and lay on the bed, and then I felt something else on my legs and I quickly got up, grabbed a blanket, shook it vig-orously, and took the blanket and my clothes out to the car. The motel office was dark and the vacancy sign was out. It was nearly midnight. There was no way that I would sleep in that bed.

I curled up in the back seat and was almost asleep when I heard the car pull in next to mine. Looking over the edge of the seat, I saw two men approach the door of my unit. They were black shadows that paused and then pushed the door open. I had left it unlocked. The room light snapped on and I crouched on the floor of the car, not daring to breathe. It was a few minutes before the room light went off. I waited. Would they look inside my Toyota, find me hugging the floor of the back seat and drag me out? Then the engine of the car next to me started and they drove off.

Shit, I thought. Whoever it is knows where I am. Whoever it is has the ability to find me a thousand fucking miles from my house. This person is more than some Hispanic thug at my doorstep. I put on my clothes and pulled out of the motel parking lot onto the highway. I would go to Fort Collins and I would find out who this fucking Luther was. Or maybe I would go back to California and put an ad in the paper:

Found: some negatives that you would like to get back and I would like to give them to you. Meet me in the coffee shop at Broadway and Bolinas and you can have the fucking things. Please give me back my negative files and my life.

I explained to the guard at the Fort Collins gate that I was looking for the Public Information Office. My car was searched, he examined my driver's license and I was given directions to a large building with clapboard sides, a relic of earlier army days. There was a statue of a horse, rust-colored, and a sign that read, *IV Army Corp, The Iron Horse.*

I found the public information office and asked the soldier at the desk who I could speak to regarding information about some 4th Army soldiers who had served in Viet Nam.

"What kind of information?" he asked.

I took out the photograph of the five soldiers and laid it on the counter. "These five guys served in Viet Nam in 1966 or 1967. I know the names of two of them, but I'd like to get the names of the other three."

He picked up a phone and spoke to someone and a young lieutenant approached the counter.

"How can I help you?" he asked.

"This photo. It was taken in Viet Nam in 1966 or 1967, and I know the names of two of the men, but I need to know the names of the three others."

"Why?"

"I'm working on a book of photographs taken by Aaron Sturgis, a photographer who took this and some other pictures in Viet Nam. He photographed Korea and Kosovo and I'm the editor of the book. At least two of these men are dead, but I'd like to find one other man who could tell me what was happening when Sturgis took his photos."

"They were 4th Army?"

"Yes. I know that two of them trained here at Fort Collins."

"They all would have trained here if they were Ivy." The word was puzzling and then I realized that the Roman numeral IV had been on the sign out in front. Ivy. The IV Army.

"It would be like looking for a needle in a haystack," he said. "Five guys in half a squad more than forty years ago. I'll tell you what. You get your publisher to put your request in writing and send it to me and I'll get permission for a search. Have them send me a copy of the photograph and the names you have so far."

"I can do that," I said, and I thanked him for his time.

I had struck out. Nothing left to do except drive back to California and wait for someone to collect the negatives. I could give them to the messenger from God if he showed up again. Or give them to Emma Sturgis and let the light shine on her. I could leave the manila envelope on a table in my front room with a big sign on the front door that said, **The door is**

unlocked, and they're inside on the table. Please don't break anything.

And I could kiss my ten years of negative files goodbye.

I took my time getting back to California. I slept in the car at rest stops and ate fast food from drive-throughs and managed to get back to Fairfax with twenty dollars still in my wallet.

But when I opened the door of the house, I was met with a scene that was familiar. Someone had been in the house and had torn it apart again. And then it dawned on me that it wasn't the same searchers as before. They had already been through the house. This had to be somebody else, and that meant that more than one person wanted to find those negatives. It was too late to put a sign on the door.

The restaurant was called Il Davide and it was on A Street in San Rafael. There were six tables on the sidewalk under the street trees, and on summer days they filled up in the afternoon. All I wanted was a cool place with a chilled glass of sauvignon blanc. The small bar just inside the door would be empty at two o'clock and I would be out of sight. I came out of the parking garage and was about to turn into the restaurant when I saw her, sitting at one of the sidewalk tables.

She wore a red top with slender straps and her fingernails were blood red. There were red teardrops in her ears and her lips were glossy red. When she leaned forward, I saw the almost-curve of her breasts and the sharpness of her cheekbones and the shine of her forehead in the sun. I was suddenly aware that she was the portrait of Emma Sturgis, only this was a real woman, my age, with the same exotic beauty that was in the Paris photograph. Someone had cloned the twenty-year-old Emma Sturgis.

"Hello Michael," she said. She motioned to the empty chair opposite.

I sat. "You know my name," I said.

"Yes."

"But I don't know your name. Would it be a wild guess if I said you were the daughter of Emma Sturgis?"

"Olivia Sturgis."

"The long-lost daughter."

"My mother told you that?"

"She said you had disconnected from her. That she had no idea where you were."

"My mother has difficulty with the truth."

"You mean she's a liar."

"Not always. Sometimes she knows it's a lie but more often she changes things to fit her own desires. And believes her version."

"How do you know me?"

"Right now you're a person that several people are interested in."

"People who know I have some negatives that belonged to your father?"

"That's right."

"So how did you know I would be here this afternoon?"

"I followed you. I was waiting at your house but you opened your front door, stood there a moment, and then went back to your car. I had no chance. And while you were taking your time in the parking garage, I parked on the street." She pointed to a small car at a meter a few yards away. "And then I parked myself here at this table where you wouldn't miss me. And right now what I'd like would be a glass of wine."

"Like mother, like daughter."

Her face clouded. "No. You have that one wrong. I may look like her, but the resemblance stops there."

I ordered two glasses of wine. She said nothing nor did I while we waited for them. When they were set in front of us, she raised hers to touch mine. "Cheers," she said.

"That's not what your mother said when she did this."

"I can guess what she said."

"Why would your mother tell me you had disappeared?"

"It probably suits something she has in mind. She doesn't do things without reason."

"And why have you tracked me down?"

"When my father was dying, he told me about those negatives. But he died and no one knew where they were until you showed up at Fosberg's shop with a photograph of my mother."

"And you want them?"

"You and I have a mutual interest in those negatives."

"My only interest is in getting them to somebody so that they stop trashing my house and threatening me. I thought it was one person, but now it appears there are two of them."

"And you don't know who to give them to."

"I asked your mother who it might be, but she said she didn't know."

"That's entirely possible. My father may never have given her a name."

"And you? Do you know?"

"I know this. For years someone has deposited a substantial check in my mother's bank account every month. She always claimed it was the result of clever investments, but my father, before he died, told me that it was connected to some negatives. He said that once he was dead, the checks would stop. That his last act would be to give the negatives to the person who sent the checks. My mother is a piece of work, Michael. My father never got the chance to send off the negatives. His cancer took over, he became comatose, and then he was dead."

"Why did he want to give the negatives back?"

"He was a freelancer all his life. There were long periods when he made no money, but those checks kept my mother and me alive. He told me there was no point in keeping them any longer, but his lights went out and the negatives were hidden. My mother turned everything upside down. She looked for a safety deposit box or a key, looked everywhere. And then you turned up with them."

"Were you and your father close?"

"No. He was rarely there when I was growing up. He was always off at some war or some insurrection. When he came home, he and my mother were like fireworks, sex and shouting matches, banging doors, fucking, and the opera and late dinners and days when I never saw them. But when he was gone, she lived her own life."

"Bill Fosberg said she collected men."

"Bill Fosberg is a nasty old gossip. But he knew about the negatives, too."

"Why are you telling me this?"

She raised the glass of wine to sip at it. Her hand rose to her chest and she pressed it to her skin in the same motion that was in the photograph of her mother in Paris, and I thought, Jesus fucking Christ, there's no way we can avoid the genetics that shape us. I watched her hand move across her skin and it was hard to concentrate on her words.

"Because you have those negatives."

"And you want them."

"Yes."

"Why should I trust you any more than I trust your mother?"

"Because I've just told you something you don't know about them, and I know how to turn them into gold."

"I'm only interested in keeping somebody from trashing my darkroom, and I want back ten years of negatives that represent a fucking lot of creative work."

"And I think we can get them back."

"You tell me your mother is a liar and that Bill Fosberg is a nasty old gossip. Somebody sent a thug to my house in the middle of the night and two days ago men searched a motel in Colorado when they thought I was there. Somebody murdered two Viet Nam veterans in Texas, and your father stuck that in there along with some photographs that are fucking horrific. Why should I trust you?"

She leaned forward again and she was amazingly beautiful, and I was aware of the fact that she knew what she was doing, and I thought, if you fall down the well, Michael, this would not be the worst thing that could happen to you. You might drown, but your last breath could be a spectacular one.

"Because you don't have a lot of choices. You can go back to your house and wait for them to come. Or you and I can sort this out and when it's all done you'll be on easy street."

It was suddenly tempting. I would never have to photograph some ugly woman and her crazy dogs again, I thought. No more whining children or women who want me to take twenty years off their lives or men who want me to reverse their receding hairline.

"Tell me about the negatives, Michael."

"You have no idea what they are?"

"All my father said was that they were terribly important to someone And that someone has put money in a bank account since I was a child. I went to college on that money."

"There's one photo of five men in Viet Nam. I know the names of some of them. I went to Texas to talk to the sister of one of them."

"Which explains why you haven't been home for a week."

"You've been looking for me?"

"You were gone and Bill Fosberg's shop has been shut up, too."

"Not unusual. Sometimes he doesn't open for days."

"So maybe you disappearing and his shop closing are a coincidence?"

"I have no idea. He couldn't have known where I was going. Nobody knew." And in the back of my mind I could see the dark shadows of those men entering the motel room in Colorado.

"What about the other negatives?" she asked.

"One of your mother. That photo hangs on the wall of her house. One of a painting of a scene in Texas. That was how I found the woman who told me two of the names and half of another one. And some Viet Nam photos of men committing an atrocity."

"Bingo," she said. "All we have to do is match one of those guys with the money."

"And now the pronoun is *we*?"

"You have the negatives. I know how to find the name."

I was suddenly hungry. "I need something to eat," I said. "You want lunch?"

"Does this mean you're with me on this?"

"Let's say I'm sticking my toe in the water. I need to find out if there are any alligators lurking in there."

"I'm not the alligator," she said. "They've already been to your house. Twice."

She raised the glass of wine and sipped, setting it back on the small white table. A breeze stirred the hanging leaves of the pepper tree at the edge of the curb. The waiter set a plate on the table of the couple next to us. It had chunks of yellow beet and thin crostini with prosciutto and she eyed it. "That looks good," she said. She looked back at me and waited.

She raised one hand to pull her hair back from her face. The waiter had disappeared. She rose and went inside the restaurant and came back a minute later with napkins, silver, and two glasses of water.

"Anything else, sir?" she asked as she sat.

"What time do you get off?" I joked.

"I never date the customers," she said. "But I was a waitress while I was in college," she added. "Did I embarrass you by bringing out the table setups?"

"No," I said.

The waiter came out and set a square white plate in front of us. Arranged on it were a dozen thin slices of roasted beet and two crostini with goat cheese and a wafer-thin piece of prosciutto.

"When did we order this?" I asked.

"I said it looked good," she said. "So when I was inside I ordered it." The beets tasted of vinegar and olive oil. And it was as good as it had looked.

She had gone inside, ordered the food, and had come out with silverware and water. She was not someone who was afraid of being thought of as pushy, that was for sure. Not like the last woman I had been seeing.

My latest disaster was an elementary school teacher, in her thirties, attractive, funny, and I liked her a lot. We went to the museum together and joked about what painting we would steal for each other, and she seemed genuinely interested in my photographs.

I asked her to come to lunch so that I could take some photographs of her. We had cracked crab and a chilled chardonnay on the little porch in the back of my house. The sun was hot and I asked her to pose for me.

"But you need to take off your clothes," I had said. It wasn't that we had not been intimate. And I had seen her naked any number of times. But the idea of photographs made her nervous.

"Nobody will see these except you and me," I said.

"I know you," she said. "If they're any good, they'll end up hanging on a wall someplace where the whole world can see them."

But she posed for me, wearing an old white shirt of mine, the collar frayed, a few buttons missing, and the photographs were more than I could have hoped for. There was one of her sitting in an old chair, wearing nothing but the unbuttoned shirt, one breast partially exposed, and her expression was pure joy, a freakish delight that leaped off the paper when I printed it.

When I showed it to her, she said, "That's not me!"

"But it is you," I said.

"No," she said, and she took the print and tore it in half. "That's not me," she repeated.

And that was the end of that relationship. There were half a dozen photographs from that session that ended up pinned to my darkroom wall. I tried calling her several times, but she was busy; no, she couldn't make it to dinner on Tuesday; no, Saturday she was having lunch with some other teachers at the museum, planning a field trip. Maybe next week. Give me a call. But it was obvious that next week would be filled, too, so

I didn't call. But I had those photographs on the wall of my darkroom. And they were good. And I wished that she had said to me, "Oh, Michael, that's me!" But she hadn't said that.

Now, across from me sat a beautiful woman in a red top with bare shoulders and I thought, I still have that old white shirt. And she had already used the pronoun *we*.

"Come on, Michael," she said. She was leaning forward, and she reached one hand across the table to press onto mine. "Either you get beat up by a bunch of thugs and they take the negatives, or we turn them into cash."

"I think there's two people who want them. Somebody searched my house again while I was in Texas."

She continued to hold my hand. "Doesn't matter," she said. "All we want is the guy with the money."

"What makes you so hot to do this?" I asked. "It's not without substantial risk."

"I think of it as my father's legacy. All I got out of him was a check to my mother that paid the rent and allowed her to live a lifestyle that, when I was a teenager, was quite frankly embarrassing. And it never seemed to bother him. He came home from some war and the two of them became another embarrassment. I figure I'm owed this." Her voice had grown in intensity and her grip on my hand had tightened.

"How are you going to find the names?" I asked. "Three of those guys are dead. I only have a first name for one of the others."

"Two things," she said. "You need to go someplace with those negatives where they can't find you. And I'm going to spend some time with an old boyfriend who works in a bank. I'm going to weasel the name of the guy who sent those checks to my mother's account."

"You won't get the name. Banks don't divulge such things."

"Trust me," she said. "I can do that. You keep the negatives safe." She picked up a crostini and bit off the end of it. She wasn't shy about eating, either.

"So I go hide in a cave somewhere until you call me?"

"Can you find some place a bit more comfortable?"

"Yes," I said. "I know of a place. It's maybe six hours from here. In the Sierras."

"So you go back to your house and you pack up a few things, and then disappear."

"I went to Texas and they found me in Colorado. Whoever it is, has a net that spreads pretty wide."

"Drive to the airport. Park in the long-term parking lot. Go to the terminal. Get yourself lost in the crowd. They won't worry about it. If they can find you in Colorado, they can find your name on an airline manifest. But you go to Hertz or Avis. Rent a car. You'll be long gone by the time they discover you never flew anywhere."

"This isn't new to you, is it?"

"Let's say I've thought it out pretty carefully."

"There are no phones where I'm going."

She pushed her napkin across the table. "Write down the directions," she said. "It will take me at least a day on my end. And then I'll come and get you and we'll close the deal."

"I doubt if it will be that simple. I doubt if these people will simply dump money on us and go away."

"Once they have the negatives, we're no longer interesting."

"I printed them. They'll assume that."

"Prints are no good. They can be doctored. They can be from anywhere. But a strip of negatives, taken at the same time, that's what's dangerous and that's what they want."

Her hand was against the skin of her chest, sliding under the strap of the red top, and I thought again of her mother and I thought, Oh, fuck it, Michael. Climb on board the roller coaster and don't shut your eyes.

I was in my darkroom packing my camera bag when I heard the front door open. My first thought was that it was Olivia, but then I thought, oh shit, here's no reason for her to come here, and I turned toward the darkroom door as it opened.

It was Cindy Piper's old man, the boxer shorts guy from Texas. But this time he was dressed: old tennis shoes, a pair of dirty Levis, a faded blue chambray work shirt, and a frayed denim jacket. He wore aviator sunglasses, big ones that covered a third of his face, but I knew it was him. The pock-marked skin and the ominous presence were unmistakable.

"Remember me?" he said.

It would have been hard to forget that voice.

"You're a long way from home," I said.

"Thirty-six hours. Couple of stops for a piss, gas, and here I am."

"Why?"

"Day after you talked to Cindy a guy showed up asking about you. Wanted to know what Cindy told you. Wanted to know what kind of a picture you showed her. He was a bit of a problem."

"What kind of a problem?"

"He gimme some cash like you did, and he talked to Cindy and she told him she didn't want to talk no more. She told him she had the picture you give to her and he wanted to see it but she said no, and she went back inside the house. He wanted to come inside the fence. Remember the fence? And my dogs?"

I said nothing.

"Yeah, I'll bet you 'member my dogs. So he goes back to his car and he comes back with a pair of bolt cutters, and he tells me, let me inside the goddamn gate or I'll cut the fucking thing open, and I said, you do that and I'll feed you to my dogs, and then he pulls out a gun and he shoots one of the dogs."

"Then what happened?"

"Next body they pull out of the Trinity River is gonna have a hole in the forehead and all the brains leaked out."

"Who was he?"

"Some asshole who thought I was a dumb cracker he could jerk around."

"What did he look like? Was he one of the men in the photograph?"

"He was a short Mexican. Built like a brick shithouse."

"Wore a Carhartt jacket?"

"Somebody you know?" he asked.

"I saw him once. He came here."

"But he didn't shoot one of your dogs, did he?"

"You shot him and dumped him in the river?"

"Seemed like the logical thing to do." The voice was slow and measured.

"So why did you come here?"

"Because it looks to me like the hunnert dollars you give me to talk to Cindy is a drop in the bucket. Somebody wants to talk to Cindy and see that picture that bad and he gives me a hunnert dollars too, I smell real money."

"Why would I have money to give to you?"

"Hard to say. Cindy says her brother talked about something that happened in Viet Nam and he could never tell her what it was, but he was gonna talk to somebody and then he ended up in that river. And his buddy, Ronnie, he got dumped there not long after. The cops didn't do nothing. Just two old drunk vets; but I'm thinking, here comes some pretty boy from California with a picture of Chip and Ronnie, and then here comes some hard-case beaner with a gun, and there's something up and I smell money. Might be worth checking it out."

"How did you find me?"

He fished in his jacket pocket and took out the business card I had given to Cindy. "You was kind enough to give us your address. I guess it would have been polite to call ahead. Let you know you was going to have company. But I forgot to do that."

"I've got nothing for you. And this time you aren't inside your fence with your dogs and a gun."

"I got one of them dogs in my truck." He reached into the denim jacket again and pulled out the gun.

"What is it they say on TV? Never leave home without it?"

"But you're not going to shoot me because if you do, anything you want to know or any money that you might get would disappear."

"You may be pretty, but you're not stupid. I'll give you that. But I could make you ugly quicker'n you could say, 'don't put my eye out.' Or something like that."

"I don't have any money and I don't know who those guys in the photograph are, so you've wasted your time coming up here."

"But when you do find out, you're going to cash in, aren't you." It wasn't a question, simply a statement of fact. "So I figure that you'll lay your hands on some money to get rid of me. I'm your worst nightmare, and you're hoping you'll wake up." He paused, and then he said, "You got a nice house here. Must be worth something."

"It's not mine. I rent it from an old lady who lives in San Rafael."

"I'll bet you got a whole lot of shit in this house you could turn into money." He reached over and picked up my Rollei from the table next to the door. "What's this worth?"

"It's an old camera. Not much."

"Bullshit. Maybe you and me could go to some camera store and see what it's worth. There must be one of them places around here."

"It's not worth that much," I repeated.

"You and that beaner got something in common. You both think I'm some dumb cracker that don't know shit. I'll bet you could get a grand for this, easy." He set the camera back on the table. And he was right. Fosberg would give me two thousand and think it was a bargain. On eBay I could get three.

"How about it, pretty boy? What would Luther's last name be worth to you?"

"Luther who?"

He raised the pistol, pointed it straight at my chest and his voice became hard.

"Don't fuck with me, you California pussy. You know goddamn well who I'm talking about. Cindy remembered Luther's last name. He's one of them dudes in that photograph, which you goddamn do remember. You want that name or do you want me to fix it so you have trouble walking?" He lowered the gun so that it pointed directly at my right knee.

"No cell phone reception in the canyon," he said. "Call me from Truckee." Skinner was stretched out on the couch in the living room.

"We ready to roll?" he asked.

I told him about my plan to go to the airport and rent a car to throw anyone off my tail. Skinner laughed.

"If they're going to foller you that won't stop them. We got my little friend here." He tucked his gun into the waistband of his pants and pulled the jacket over it.

"We go in my car?" I asked.

"You go in your car, I follow in my truck. I don't feel comfortable in somebody else's vehicle."

"You don't know where we're going."

"Don't make no difference. You won't lose me."

And I didn't. His truck was two lengths behind me for the next two hours on the Interstate, and when we passed Sacramento and began to climb into the Sierras, he closed the distance so that all I could see was the grill. We stopped in Auburn to buy groceries that I put in a cooler in the trunk of my car. Skinner never left my side. It was getting dark when I swung off Highway 70 onto the graveled road that led to the resort. At the bottom of the hill where the road crossed the Middle Fork of the Feather River there was a gate at the bridge. In the headlights I twisted the combination lock and swung the gate open. When I looked back, there was the beat-up pickup, the black outline of Skinner behind the wheel, the shorter lump on the passenger side that was his dog.

Below me the river was dark, only the white of the rapids visible in the reflected headlights. I pointed to the gate, made some motions with my hands to show Skinner that he was to close the gate after he had come onto the bridge. I got back in my car and drove to the far side of the bridge and waited. In the rear view mirror I saw his truck dip onto the bridge, then stop and his dark figure got out to close the gate. We drove onto the road that paralleled the river for a quarter of a mile until we came to the black shapes of the cabins. Each cabin had a name: Trout, Bear, Blue Jay. The one we would be staying in was named Squirrel and it was the last cabin, tucked away among the huge jack pines.

It was a low-slung cabin with a rusted tin roof, a weathered screen door, and a sloping wooden floor. There was a heater in the wall, and I remembered a gas flame bubbling in it from a propane tank outside, but I knew that this time the gas had been turned off. The shower and toilet were in a lean-to scabbed onto the north wall.

Skinner followed me into the cabin. I flipped the switch and the single bulb in the center of the ceiling glowed. He looked at the bed that filled most of the room.

"Where you gonna sleep?" he asked.

"On that bed."

"No. that's where I sleep," he said. He went on through into the tiny kitchen. "Maybe you could sleep back here," came his voice.

"You sleep in the cabin next door," I said. "It's the same as this one. It's named Skunk. Ought to be just right for you."

"You think maybe I'll sleep there and you can get in your car and drive off and leave me in this shithole?"

"Park your truck behind my car."

"I already done that. When does this partner of yours show up?"

"I don't know. Maybe tomorrow, maybe two or three days from now."

"You got anything to drink in that cooler of food?"

"A bottle of scotch."

"Sounds about right," he said. He went out to his truck and came back with the dog. It was one of the dogs that had been at the fence in Texas, but without its companions it was calm. The hair on the back of its neck rose when it saw me but it stayed next to Skinner.

"He sleeps on the porch," Skinner said. "You got to step over him to go anyplace. He don't like that."

Skinner went out to my car, opened the trunk and lifted out the cooler. He took out the bottle of scotch, got a blanket from his truck, and went into the cabin next door. But all was not lost. I had the remains of a pint of scotch that I had stuffed, at the last minute, into my camera bag. I got the rest of my things out of the car, brought the cooler into the kitchen, took out some ice and poured the last of the pint into a glass. When I opened the front door, the dog, lying on the small porch, sat up and growled. I went to the kitchen and stepped out the back door. Somewhere lightning lit up the sky briefly. A storm was passing through and the air was moist. I heard the distant rumble of thunder. I sipped at my drink and wondered what would happen next. Would Olivia show up? Would the people stalking me find where I was? Somehow the idea that Skinner was in the cabin next door with his gun was reassuring.

There was a brilliant flash and the crack! of thunder closer and then the rain came, a sudden downpour. I went back into the cabin. Rain drummed on the roof for a few minutes, slowed and stopped, and I slept. It was silent when I woke again. The long whistle of a diesel engine in the canyon had awakened me. A train was laboring up the grade and it grew louder until it throbbed from across the river and then faded. I lay awake wondering what it would be like to run alongside a freight train, clamber into an empty boxcar and ride east into Nevada. Go somewhere no one could find me. The rain began again, a steady white noise on the tin roof. I fell asleep and dreamed that I was in a house with many rooms. I kept opening doors, trying to find a way out, but every door I opened led to another room. When I awoke and looked at my watch it was four o'clock and the rain had slowed to a soft beat.

Skinner was sitting on the little porch with his dog when I opened the door the next morning. He turned to me and said, "Eggs over easy. Coffee."

"You think this is a restaurant?" I said.

"You gonna feed yourself and you gonna feed us," he said, absently scratching the dog's neck.

"So how does he like his eggs?"

"Raw. But he don't drink coffee."

I went back into the kitchen and broke three eggs into a bowl. I fried eggs and made toast for the two of us, and by the time they were cooked, the coffee was ready.

"Like I said, you gonna make somebody a good wife," he said, taking the plate from me. He scooped the eggs onto the toast with his fingers, took the other piece of toast and mashed it on top, making a sandwich. The egg yolks dripped between his legs onto the edge of the porch and the dog pushed his head in to lick up the spill. When Skinner was finished, he held out his hands, and the dog licked them, too.

"What is the name?" I asked.

"You mean my dog?"

"I mean the name of the man in the photograph. The one Cindy remembered."

"You are a persistent little cunt," he said. "The name Andros mean anything to you?"

"Is that the name?"

"That's what Cindy said. Luther Andros. Is he the guy who's looking for them photographs?"

"I have no idea." In the back of my head the name Luther Andros seemed to ring a bell. It was somehow familiar, as if I had seen it some place, perhaps in a newspaper or heard it on the news. But I couldn't place it.

"Who's this partner of yours?" he asked.

"She's the daughter of the man who took the pictures."

"What's her interest?"

"None of your business."

He turned to face me. "I could have Bandit here chew off your balls. Or maybe I could just put a hole in your head like I done to that beaner and wait here for your partner myself. Or you could answer the fucking question."

"She thinks she can find out who wants the negatives and she thinks whoever it is will pay for them."

"So the dude you want is this Luther Andros?"

"Maybe. Or maybe it's the other one. The one whose name we don't know yet. But Andros would know what went on in those photographs."

"You ain't told me what's in them."

"They're from Viet Nam."

"I already figured that out. The picture you showed Cindy was from Viet Nam. So what's so fucking important about them?"

"One of them shows a soldier executing a woman and a child. Another one shows a village going up in flames. But you can't tell which one of those guys did it. Whoever it is, he doesn't want those negatives on the loose."

"So you think he'll pay a shitload of money to get them back and shut you up?"

"Something like that."

"Don't sound like you got this thought all the way through."

The dog got up and trotted over to a tree where a blue jay had perched. The dog looked up and the jay began to scream at it, sharp raw yells. The dog barked and the jay shrieked back. Skinner reached down and pulled his pistol from where it was tucked into the top of his pants. He raised it, said, "Shut the fuck up," and pulled the trigger. There was a sharp report and the jay disappeared in an explosion of feathers. Part of the carcass fell at the base of the tree and the dog pounced on it.

"You want to shut something up, that's the way you do it," he said.

The rest of the day passed quietly. I walked down to the bridge to look at the river and Skinner followed, his dog trotting at his heels. There was a hint of fall in the air, the hot afternoon followed by a sudden drop in temperature, a crispness in the air before the light softened among the trees. I cooked chicken for dinner, mixing it with vegetables in a tomato sauce and some Italian seasoning. Skinner said, "I knew it. You gonna make some bitch happy. You gonna be one of them pussy-whipped dudes who cooks dinner and runs the vacuum cleaner and apologizes every time she don't come."

"Fuck you," I said.

"Whoops! I touched a nerve in pussy-boy!"

"You still got that bottle of scotch?"

"Does a bear shit in the woods?"

"I'd like a drink."

"So would I, pussy-boy." He got up from the little table in the kitchen and went to the cabin next door, coming back a minute later with the bottle of scotch. It was half-empty. He took two glasses down from the shelf and poured a generous shot in each one. "Here's to the fucking golden goose," he said. "When it lays the egg, we gonna drink better stuff than this."

Skinner had two more drinks and the bottle was nearly empty. He held it up and said, "Is there a store someplace where you can get some more of this? Or maybe some beer?"

"There's a store in Graeagle about five miles from here. But the less anybody sees of us, the better it will be."

"Nobody knows who the fuck I am. You give me some money and I'll go get us some reinforcements."

"Aren't you afraid I'll disappear?"

"Not when your car won't start. Unless you want to hit the road and hitchhike. In which case I wait here for your partner. She worth fucking?"

Skinner took something from under the hood of my car and I watched his truck go down the narrow road past the other cabins. It was growing dark and the temperature was dropping quickly. I sat on the little porch, the pines growing black around me. Thirty minutes later I saw his headlights and he was back with another bottle of scotch, a case of beer, a big bag of corn chips and a jar of salsa.

"I got all the food groups," he announced. "Can't get along on an unbalanced diet." He popped one of the beers and held it out to me.

I shook my head. He tipped the can up and drank half of it, belched, and drank the other half, hurling the can into the woods. "So when is your partner gonna show up?" he asked.

"I told you, I don't know. Maybe tomorrow, maybe the next day."

"Maybe she don't show up at all. Maybe she's shining you on and she's gonna take the whole pie herself."

"I've got the negatives. Without those she has nothing."

"You ain't entirely clueless," he said. "Same drill as last night. Bandit keeps his eye on you." He picked up the bottle of scotch.

"I'd like some of that," I said.

"I am a generous man," he said. He poured a water glass half full and went into the cabin next door. Bandit settled onto the porch in front of the screen door. I could hear the river rushing behind the cabin and, somewhere, another train whistle.

I took a shower in the lean-to bathroom. The water was icy, but I stood in it a long time until I was so cold I could barely breathe. I crawled into my sleeping bag and shook until some of the heat came back into my body.

The next morning Skinner had his egg sandwich again, and Bandit licked his hands. Skinner had a beer with breakfast and then another, and he spent the rest of the morning drinking beer and eating corn chips and salsa and then at noon made a bologna sandwich and drank some more beer, but he never slurred or staggered. He and the dog sat in the sun, Skinner leaning against the wall of the cabin, the dog stretched out at his feet.

I thought about the blue jay. Skinner was right. The people who wanted the negatives wouldn't be satisfied to simply pay some money and turn us loose. Two of the soldiers in that photograph had been murdered. I had been tracked all the way to Colorado and my house had been ransacked. And he was right about something else. I hadn't thought this all the way through. I wasn't sure Olivia had, either.

Skinner was on his second case of beer and second bottle of scotch when Olivia arrived the following day. I went into the little kitchen for a drink of water and she was standing there, just inside the back door. She held one finger up to her lips and motioned me toward the door. We slipped outside and went down through the trees to the edge of the river.

"Who's the man on the front porch?"

"A bad dream," I said. "He's the man who lives with Cindy Piper, the woman in Texas who had a brother in that photograph."

"What's he doing here?"

"Long story," I said.

"I parked my car across the bridge. The gate was locked and I walked in and when I saw the truck I was careful and then I saw him and the dog. What's he want?"

"He wants a piece of the action," I said. "He carries a gun and he's used it. Not here, but in Texas."

"Why did you bring him here?"

"I had no choice."

"My car is outside the gate. We could get in it and leave him here."

"The negatives are inside in my camera bag."

"Get them,'" she said. "I'll meet you at the car," and she started along the edge of the river toward the bridge. I went back up to the cabin, entering the back door into the kitchen. Skinner was standing there, eating another bologna sandwich.

"You take a hike in the woods?" he said.

"I went outside to take a leak."

"We need some more ice," he said, closing the cooler. "Unless your partner shows up."

I pushed past him into the other room, went over to the corner where my camera bag was and set it on the bed. I would pretend I was taking out a camera in order to take some photographs, slip the negatives into a pocket and, hopefully, convince Skinner that I was simply killing time by taking pictures. But when I opened the camera bag, the manila envelope was gone.

"You've been in my bag," I said.

"Now what would I be doing that for?" he said, standing in the doorway to the kitchen, leaning against the doorjamb. "You missing something?"

"Where are they?"

"Them pictures and them negatives? Is that what you're looking for?"

"I was looking for some film and my camera, but there's a manila envelope missing. Where is it?"

"I got to have some leverage here, pussy-boy. But don't you worry. They's safe and sound." He dropped the rest of his sandwich on the floor and Bandit gobbled it up.

I was stuck. Without the negatives, Olivia and I had nothing. She would wait at her car but there was no point in my trying to meet her without the negatives. When I didn't show, she would know something was wrong. On the other hand, without the other name, Skinner had nothing. All he had was a bargaining chip with Olivia and me. Where had he put the negatives? In his truck? Under his mattress?

"So what are you going to do when my partner shows up?"

"What's the name of that TV program? Let's make a deal? That's what we'll do."

I took the Leica out of the bag. "I'm going to go take some pictures," I said.

"What for?"

"It's what I do."

"You be back in time to make me some supper, sweetie-pie. Bandit and me would like a nice big steak and maybe some pie. You know how to make a pie, faggy-boy?"

"Fuck you," I said, opening the screen door and stepping out onto the porch. He followed.

"That ain't on my schedule," he said. "But if I get horny enough you might be in some danger." He laughed and I could feel him watching me as I went down the road past his cabin toward the bridge.

There was no car on the opposite side of the bridge. I walked out to the middle and waited. The river was dark green, half of the water in shadow, the other half still lit by the sun. Somewhere up on the highway a logging truck labored up grade, and I knew that Olivia could see me and that she was puzzled by the fact that I stood in the middle of the bridge, not trying to hide myself, in no hurry to cross to the gate. I waited.

Then I saw her, a small figure on the road leading down to the bridge, at the edge of the trees, standing, motioning to me. I thought briefly about crossing to join her. We could simply throw the whole scheme away and drive off, but I knew that she was not about to do that. The intensity in her voice when she had said the negatives were her legacy had told me that she was not about to abandon the ship. She would bargain with Skinner. She would give him a small share and perhaps I would get something, too, but I had the feeling that I was about to be the odd man out. Skinner had pointed it out to me. He had the leverage. I no longer did. And I wasn't sure I cared.

I raised the camera and pointed it at Olivia and clicked the shutter. She stepped out of the shadows and started down the road and I took another picture every ten yards. It would be an interesting sequence, I thought. Woman approaching a bridge.

When she got to the gate she ducked under it and walked to the middle of the bridge.

"What's going on, Michael?"

"Skinner. That's the man at the cabin. He has the negatives. I don't have them any longer."

"Jesus Christ! How did you let that happen?"

"I got careless. I underestimated him."

"Does he know about me?"

"He knows that I have a partner who is coming here and she may have a name that will tell us who the pictures point to."

"I don't have the name yet."

"He has one. He says one of the men is named Luther Andros."

She reached out and put her hand on my arm, pulled me toward her. "Luther Andros?"

"The name sounds familiar."

"Oh, Sweet Jesus," she said. "Luther Andros!"

"Who is he?"

"He was the Attorney General for the State of Illinois. Heavy into politics. He was the man who was the special counsel for that investigation into the Pentagon scandal. Don't you remember?"

"Vaguely."

"Your friend has given us a gift, Michael. But we can't let him know how much of a gift it is."

"He's hardly a friend, Olivia. He's a crude, rather dirty pig, but he's no dummy. You won't like him."

"There's nothing to like, Michael. Money talks. My guess is that he'll be willing to listen." She turned back toward the gate. "Unlock that, will you? I'll get my car and we can have a talk with your Texas pig."

She walked back to the gate, ducked under it and went up the graveled road. I found the lock and turned the dial: 45, 38, 22. Fred's three favorite guns. I wished I had one of them.

Skinner stood and lifted the pistol from his waistband as Olivia turned the car against the porch. He waited, the pistol at his side, his dog standing next to him while Olivia and I got out. As Olivia came around the front of the car, he looked first at her, then at me and said, "Holy shit. You just went up about a hundred notches, pussy boy. And you, sweet lady, you might be the best fucking looker I ever seen."

"Somebody ought to wash out your mouth," Olivia said. "No need to be that vulgar." She stood in front of the car, and I heard the click as Skinner put the safety back on the pistol. Olivia was dressed in jeans and a white shirt, and she reached up with both hands to pull her hair back, lifting it off the back of her neck. As she did so, the shirt pressed against her breasts and lifted so that her slender hips became apparent, and I thought we should have turned the car around at the gate and gone far from here, far from this crude man and his nasty dog.

"Michael tells me you have the negatives," she said.

"Well. You get right to it, don't you? Don't waste no time. I'll bet you're quick about some other things, too."

"I'm going to pretend you didn't say that. Those negatives aren't worth anything to you," she said. "You need us to turn them into something worthwhile."

"And what would you have that would do that? I got the negatives and the pictures and I got the names of some of the boys in that picture. Two of them was murdered and another one died in 'Nam and I got another name. Won't take much to find out who else is there. Unless you got the missing piece of the puzzle."

"Which you don't get," she said. "You like to shoot things, don't you?"

Skinner raised the pistol and pointed it at me.

"Think of it this way," Olivia said. "You have the pistol. But you don't have the bullets or anybody to shoot them at. And that's what I have."

Skinner clicked the safety off. "I could shoot him right now," he said. "That would make one less to share with. Or maybe you could tell me what you know and then I don't shoot him."

"I don't think you're going to do that," Olivia said. "You can hold out for thirty percent of something, or you can pull the trigger and get one hundred percent of nothing. You need me. I need him. That's the way it works."

"So what happens now?" Skinner asked, lowering the gun to his side. The safety was still off.

"Tomorrow we drive to Reno. We leave Michael's car here. We check ourselves into one of those great big anonymous casino hotels. I need a place where my lap top works and I need a phone. My guess is you'll stick close to us because you need us as much as we need those negatives."

"So, pussy-boy," he said to me. "Time for a drink? I think your lady friend here has more balls than you got." He raised the pistol again and aimed it at the front tire of Olivia's car. He pulled the trigger and the tire went flat. He turned to my car and shot again.

"We go in my truck," he said. "Three of us fit in the front seat, Bandit rides in the back. Be a bit cozy but you won't mind that, will you, sweetie?"

Olivia joined me in the kitchen while I made some spaghetti. She held out a glass with some scotch in it and said, "Here. You need this more than I do."

"We're screwed, aren't we?" I said. "We can't get rid of him and you said you didn't have the other name."

"But we have Luther Andros. And when we get to Reno and I plug into the Internet, I can find how we get in touch with Andros. He's got to know about the negatives. And he'll know who the other guy is. It's either Andros or the mystery man who pulled the trigger on that woman and child. And one of them has wanted silence all these years."

"But there's somebody else, Olivia. Somebody else took my house apart the second time."

"Which would be somebody who wants those negatives to blackmail Andros or his buddy. Either way, they're worth a great deal."

"So we go to Reno tomorrow with Skinner?"

"We have no choice. But at least we know that the negatives are right next to us. How did he find you?"

"I left my card with Cindy Piper. Told her to call me if she remembered anything else. She remembered Luther's last name and Skinner smelled the money."

"It doesn't matter. Maybe we'll have to cut him in for a piece."

"You offered him a third."

"A third of what? It's a third of whatever I say it is."

We ate the spaghetti on the front porch. There was a bowl of spaghetti for Bandit. He didn't growl at Olivia. It was dark when we finished and Skinner stood, picked up the half-empty scotch bottle, put his arm around Olivia, and squeezed her breast with his hand.

"You want a real man, little lady, you know where to find me," and he stepped off the porch toward his cabin.

Inside our cabin Olivia said, "Is there a shower?"

"There is. But the water is cold, There's no heat."

"I don't care. I want to wash his stink off me."

I showed her the shower and she stripped off her shirt, stepped out of her jeans. She unsnapped her bra, dropping it on top of her shirt and jeans, slid her panties down, and left her clothes in a puddle on the floor.

"You can join me and help scrub the last half hour away if you want."

There was a shriek as she stepped under the icy water, but I couldn't feel it as I stepped in beside her. She held out the soap and I lathered her back, her buttocks, her shoulders, bent to run my slippery hands down her legs.

When she turned, she put her arms around me and pulled me into her. "I like you Michael," she said. The water ran down our faces and she kissed me and said, "Maybe we'll take the money and go where nobody can find us."

"Are you serious?" I asked.

"You never know," she said. "I might change my mind. And then, again, I might not."

I toweled her off and we crawled into the bed and held each other until feeling came back to our bodies.

"Yes, you can," she whispered.

That was when we heard someone at the front door. My first thought was that it was Skinner. He would be drunk by now and he would want to fuck Olivia and I had no weapon. I slid out of bed, felt my way to the kitchen and picked up the heavy knife I had used to cut the bread. At that moment I heard someone at the back door. Which meant that it wasn't Skinner. He couldn't be in two places at once. I went back into the front room and stood in the dark next to the door. I could hear the screen open, and then the wooden door swung inward. But the person outside didn't come in. He stood just outside the doorway and he said, "Turn on the light."

It wasn't Skinner's voice.

By now the person at the back door had entered and I could see his shadowy outline in the doorway of the kitchen.

"The light," the voice repeated. "Turn the fucking light on."

I remained rooted next to the door.

Then a voice came from the man in the kitchen doorway.

"I can see you next to the front door," he said. "You do something stupid and it will be the last thing you try to do." Suddenly a flashlight beam from his direction illuminated me. I stood, naked in the light, holding the heavy kitchen knife.

Olivia's voice came from the bed.

"Turn on the light, Michael."

I pushed up the switch that was next to me on the wall. The single bulb in the ceiling went on and I saw the man in the kitchen doorway, tall, muscular, wearing boots, workpants and a heavy jacket. He held a gun in one hand and a large flashlight, the kind cops carry, in the other. The man outside the front door stepped in. He was smaller than the other man, and he wore a leather bomber jacket and polished black street shoes. His hair was close-cropped in a military style and he wore rimless glasses. He held out his hand. "Give it to me," he said. "Handle first."

I gave him the knife and he threw it across the room where it clattered against the wall. I was suddenly very cold. Olivia was sitting up in the bed, the blankets pulled up to her chin.

"We're going to do this quickly," the front door man said. "There's two of you and three vehicles. Who else is here?"

"Nobody," I said. "The truck belongs to the man who owns this place."

"It's got Texas license plates."

"I don't know anything about that," I said. "What do you want?"

"I think you know what we want. And we can do this quickly. Give us the negatives and any prints you made from them and we'll be gone."

"Who are you?"

"Nobody you would know."

"You aren't going to leave us alive," Olivia said. Her voice was level, emotionless.

"We don't have them," I said.

"Well then, you'll either tell me where they are or Bobby will have some fun with the young lady, and before he's finished my guess is that you'll remember where they are."

"It won't matter, Michael," she said. "They aren't going to leave us alive." But her voice was tremulous now, and she clutched the blankets to herself with a fierceness.

He stepped over to the bed and ripped the covers away from her.

"My, my," he said, "what an attractive package." He looked at his companion who pushed his gun into his belt, reached into his pocket and withdrew a long ivory-handled knife. It snapped open.

"It would be a shame to cut those off," the man holding the blankets said.

"Somebody else has the negatives for safe-keeping," I said.

"So you tell me who that is and I tell Bobby to curb his appetite."

Bobby crossed to the bed, reached out and touched the point of the knife to Olivia's thigh. He traced a line up toward her belly, and a thin welling of blood rose. She uttered a sharp cry and my body convulsed as if I had been the one who had been cut.

"No!" I said. "It's the guy from Texas. The one who owns the truck!"

Bobby stopped and they both turned to me.

"What man from Texas? Where is he?"

At that moment Bandit trotted into the room. The dog stopped in front of Bobby, growled, and both men, startled, turned their attention to it. And I could see, in the darkness of the kitchen, the shadow of Skinner. He had raised his gun, aiming it at the head of Bobby, and he said, "If you make any kind of a move, you're a dead man." At the sound of Skinner's voice, Bobby dropped the knife and his hand went toward his gun as he turned toward the kitchen. There was a sharp report that filled the room and Bobby pitched forward, his face blown away. Skinner turned the gun toward the other man.

"Apparently he had a hearing problem. Which is a lot worse now. But I'll bet you can hear me."

The other man stood, still holding the edge of the blanket. Olivia sat naked in the bed, and Skinner said, "Who the fuck are you?"

"Nobody you would know," the man said.

"That's no answer," Skinner said. "You got a name?"

"John."

"Well, my guess is that's not your name, but that's what I'll call you anyway. Who sent you here, John?"

"I don't know."

"Somebody sent you here. You and your deaf buddy didn't just dream this up yourselfs."

"I don't know any names."

Skinner looked at me. "Get his gun and his knife and anything in his pockets," he said, tilting his head toward the dead man. "And put on some pants. Right now you look fucking foolish."

He turned back to the other man. "Look at her," he said. "Ain't that just about the prettiest thing you ever seen? And you let your asshole buddy mark that up. You ain't got no taste for beautiful things."

Olivia had touched her hand to the thin cut and smeared the blood. She was silent, petrified, and I wanted to go to her, hold her, but I, too, was rooted to my spot by the doorway.

"I got one last question," Skinner said. "Who sent you here?"

"I told you. I don't know. All I was told was to come here and get the negatives and any pictures you had."

"Who told you that?"

"The voice on the phone."

"So your phone just rang and you picked it up and said hello and some voice told you to rent a car and come all the way up here and get some negatives and kill these people? I got that right?"

The man said nothing.

"How is it that I don't believe you?" Skinner asked.

"You can believe whatever you want."

"Right now, I believe that you are no longer of any use to me." Skinner pulled the trigger and the man's head snapped back and the body crumpled to the floor.

This would not be happening, I thought, if I had taken Graham's advice and put the negatives in his police safe. I would still be in my house, somebody else would be looking for the people who had broken in and I would not be standing here with a man who had killed three men, two of them while I watched. I was deep in quicksand and it was swallowing me.

"You ain't put your pants on yet," Skinner said to me. Blood was pooling from both bodies.

"We got to clean up this mess," he said. He turned to Olivia. "You can stay right there, sweetie. I do like looking at you. Maybe I should climb in there with you and we could watch Mikey clean things up."

"Fuck you!" Olivia said with an explosion of breath. She got out of the bed, Skinner watching her closely as she went to the bathroom and closed the door behind her.

"That," he said, "is about the finest-looking ass I ever seen. And you put some pants on. Seeing you stand there with your dick hanging out is a distraction I don't need."

He tucked the pistol into his pants, bent and took the glasses off the man, felt in his pockets. "Nothing," he said. "There won't be nothing in that other prick's pants neither." He grabbed the body by the ankles and towed it to the door. Smears of blood followed the body. He dragged it outside, off the porch and came back for the other one.

"What do we do now?" I asked. I was pulling on my pants.

"We get rid of them bodies and we drive their car some-place and let it go off the road into a gully and then we haul ass out of here."

"How did you know it was a rental car?"

"'Cause it's got an Enterprise sticker on the bumper. When I heard the car I thought maybe the dude who owns this place was coming to check things out, but I seen it was a rental car and I heard them voices and I knew they must of cut that lock off."

I looked around the room for my shoes. I was in too deep now to back out. I suddenly had a flash of a long tunnel. It was at the old Sutro Baths in San Francisco, down at the edge of the sea among the ruins of the swimming pools and bathhouses. Cut through solid rock, it was black inside, and when you entered, the booming of waves slamming against an opening halfway through was so intense that it hurt your ears. When people came to that opening and saw the ocean churning be-neath them, they usually turned back. If you went further, the tiny circle of light in the opening at the far end grew, and now it felt as if I were in that tunnel, approaching that booming chasm. I would have to walk past it, and find the light at the far end. There was no turning back.

"What do we do with the bodies?" I asked.

"I'm partial to rivers."

"This one isn't deep enough."

"Don't matter. We stick them under enough rocks, when springtime comes and the water comes up, they'll wash miles down the river and they'll just be a puzzle for some country cop to figure out. We'll be long gone by then."

I helped Skinner drag the two bodies into the trees. I found a mop in the kitchen and a bucket and swabbed the floor un-til the blood and bits of the two men were gone. I tipped the bucket of bloody water out the back door and left the bucket and mop leaning against the cabin.

Olivia had not emerged from the bathroom. I listened, but there was no sound of running water. I knocked on the door, asked if she was okay, and her muffled voice replied that she was. I told her things had been cleaned up and the door opened. She came out wrapped in towels and crossed to the bed. Skinner and the dog were still in the room.

She silently climbed into the bed and slid down until only her face showed.

"You liked doing that, didn't you!" she said to Skinner.

"I don't like it or not like it. It was necessary. I saved your bacon, sweetie. I seen guys like that before. He would just as soon cut off your tits and listen to you scream. He would of liked that part. Maybe cut off Mikey's dick just for the fun of it. I seen his kind before. I did what had to be done."

The image of the knife sliding up Olivia's skin, the thin line of blood following it rose in my head, and I was glad that he was dead, angry at myself for allowing it to happen, and a wave of impotence washed across me. Skinner must have heard me as I was about to give him up to those men, but he had said nothing. I no longer counted, and I felt helpless.

"But the second man," Olivia said. "You didn't have to shoot him."

"He was a snake. I seen lots of them, too. Cottonmouths. They don't make any noise. But they is deadly all the same"

"Now that they're dead, we can't find out who sent them."

"We wouldn't of found out anyway. What we know is that whoever it is, they got ways of finding us way off here. They got eyes and ears like we ain't got. So we need to finish this up."

It occurred to me that Olivia and I were no longer in charge. Skinner was in charge now.

"What happened to Bandit tonight? Why wasn't he on the porch when they showed up," I asked

"I heard the car. I called him in. Didn't want nobody to get surprised by him. Tomorrow morning we finish up with them two and we get on the road." He turned and left, the dog following close behind.

"What did you do with them?" Olivia asked.

"Dragged them into the woods."

"You don't seem too upset by this."

"It's like it's part of a bad movie. I keep thinking the credits will roll and the lights will go on, but of course I'm being an idiot. It isn't a movie and the lights won't go on. I've just watched Skinner kill two men and I've helped him hide the bodies. You say I don't seem upset. I think I've gone past that. Right now I feel numb."

"How do you think your movie is going to end?"

"It would be nice if it was one of those boy-gets-girl-and-they-live-happily-ever-after-on-a-beach-in-Mexico movies."

"Good luck with that one," she said. "Maybe it will, maybe it won't. Turn out the light, will you please?" she added, and she rolled over to face the wall.

I turned out the light and stepped out onto the porch. It was black and there was a faint crescent moon showing through the trees. Bandit wasn't on the porch. I walked down the road until I came to the white rental car, thirty yards past Skinner's cabin. I looked in, but there were no keys. Obviously Skinner had taken care of that. I continued walking until I came to the bridge. I walked out onto the wooden planks and looked down into the darkness, an inky black below me with the sound of the river somewhere below that, so deep I did not know where it was, running over stones and beneath the stones and deeper even than that, so deep I could not measure. I remembered

Olivia sitting in the bed, naked, while the knife touched her thigh. I remembered her voice when she had said they would not leave us alive. I remembered Skinner's measured voice when he said the man was no longer of any use to him.

The white noise of the river was constant, like a wind that was unrelenting. Skinner had said that the river would wash the bodies downstream and I knew he was right, and I pictured them rising in the Spring flood, tumbling and rolling like logs caught in the current, finally coming to rest in some eddy where a fisherman or a hunter would find them. We would be long gone by then, he had said. Skinner was a pragmatist. He obviously wasted no time thinking of what might have been or what might be. He only thought of the moment and what had to be done, and he did it without worrying about moral implications. Without Skinner I would have had the negatives, and I would have given them up to the two men. But without Skinner, Olivia and I would be dead. I don't like it and I don't *not* like it, he had said. For Skinner, it was simple: something had to be done, and he had done it.

18

When I came back to the cabin, Olivia was sitting at the little table in the kitchen. She had made coffee. She was wrapped in a blanket and she looked small.

"Where were you?" she asked.

"I went for a walk. I listened to the river."

Beyond the window the forest was dark green

"When I was a child," she said, "the dark forest was frightening."

I looked again at the blackness that was outside.

"I'm not sure I understand," I said.

"I suppose it was a child's fright. But the forest was dark and it was filled with dark things and it was the place where dark things happened."

"No," I said. "When it's dark, the trees melt into each other and it's soft and there are no wolves or bears. Only the end of the day."

"Dark things happened tonight," she said. "I was terrified. Creatures came in out of the night and they were worse than anything I could ever imagine."

She lifted her coffee mug and sipped at it, and I thought, she is sensuous, no matter what she does. The blanket had slipped down so that her shoulders were bare and I wanted to reach across the table, slip my hand down inside and cup her breast in my hand, and I looked again through the window at the forest. I imagined coyotes far above us, their long legs ranging along the ridge, their dog-like faces intent on the night.

We went back to the bed and held each other and there was the white noise, resounding through the room, penetrating the walls, filling the empty space with the rush of the river. At the first bird call. I said, "It's the nightingale."

"No," she said, "it's the lark." It was neither.

She was quiet for several minutes and I said, "Are you sleeping?"

"No," came the whispered reply. "I cannot sleep." There was a pause. "It's all right," she said. "There's nothing wrong."

I slid my hand down the curve of her hip, felt the roundness of her thigh, slipped it back up until I felt the hollow of her back.

"If I were to take a picture of you," I said, "there would be a single line that rises, the line between your legs that breaks into a vee at the base of your belly, becomes two lines. And there would be only one other mark, a crescent line here." With my finger I traced under her breast that lay flat against her chest. "Four lines," I said. "That would be enough."

I cupped her breast in my hand, touched the nipple until it hardened, bent to kiss the rise of her shoulder. The bird had stopped its song. The rush of the river enveloped us.

I did not sleep again. I got up and sat in the kitchen of the cabin and listened to trains come up the canyon, and when the window began to turn gray I made some fresh coffee and waited. There was no noise from the other room. Olivia was sleeping the sleep of the dead. Then Skinner showed up. Bandit came first, coming through the front room to the kitchen, sniffing at the floor where I had mopped up the blood of the man who had fallen there. Skinner followed.

"We got to finish up," he said.

We dragged the two bodies down to the river. Skinner decided that they should be downstream a hundred yards to make sure that nobody would accidentally find them before the Spring thaw. He found a pool where he could push them under water and we rolled rocks onto them until they were covered.

"That will do," he said.

We climbed back to the cabin where Olivia waited for us.

"Git your stuff together," he said. He tossed me the keys to the rental car.

"You foller me," he said. I followed his truck across the bridge and up onto the highway, He turned down canyon and drove for several miles before he turned off at a wide spot. He came back to the car and said, "Drive this thing to the edge. Put it in gear and get out." I did what he asked and we watched the car idle forward, tip over and hurtle down the slope into the trees.

"Good enough," he said.

"You've done this before," I said.

"I done a whole lot of things before," he replied.

Back at the cabin he put Bandit in the back of the truck, threw our bags in, and told Olivia to climb in the cab.

"You sit next to me, sweetie," he said. "I want to feel that thigh of yours next to mine. I'll be hard all the way to Reno."

"What about our cars?" she asked.

"They stay here. We get the chance, we come back for them. If we get the golden egg, we don't have to fuck with old cars."

We drove to Truckee, then turned east on the Interstate toward Reno. No one said much of anything. Olivia asked where the negatives were and Skinner said, "Right under your sweet little ass." We were approaching the Nevada line and Skinner suddenly said, "Shit!" and began to slow the truck.

"What's up?" I asked.

"Look back," he said, I looked through the rear window of the cab and saw a highway patrol car, its lights blinking red and blue, just behind us.

"Not going too fast," Skinner said. "What the fuck does he want?"

He pulled over to the shoulder. The patrol car came to a stop behind us and there was a long wait. "He's running my license plate," Skinner said. He pulled his jacket so that it covered the pistol that was jammed under his belt. Jesus, I thought. He can't kill a cop. I looked through the back window of the cab, past Bandit. The dog was standing at the tailgate of the truck, barking.

"Don't look at him," Skinner said. He was intent on the side view mirror. The cop came up alongside the truck, stopping just behind the door. He motioned for Skinner to roll down the window.

"Your license and registration, please," he asked. Skinner got out his wallet and pulled out a dog-eared license. He pointed to the glove compartment. I opened it and pulled out the papers that had been crammed into it. Skinner took them, and finally selected a single sheet, handing it to the cop.

"What's the problem, Officer?" he asked.

"Your dog. California law says the dog has to be tethered if it's in the back of an open truck."

"Not in Texas," Skinner said.

"You're not in Texas now, Mister Skinner. You're in California."

"Is this going to cost me?" Skinner asked.

"I'm going to give you a break. If you can find a length of rope in your truck and tie your dog in, then you can be on your way. Another mile and you would have been in Nevada anyway."

Skinner opened the door and slid out. The cop stood a few paces back, his hand resting lightly on his holster. "You folks stay right there," he said to Olivia and me.

I thought about calling out to him, spilling everything, warning him that Skinner had a gun, but I knew that we were in too deep. I would have to keep on marching through the tunnel and hope that the light at the end was some kind of salvation.

Skinner went to the back of the pickup and began to rummage in the trash that had collected at the tailgate. He came up with a length of clothesline and he said to the cop, "This okay?"

"Looks fine to me."

Olivia's voice was barely audible. "Keep an eye on him." She bent forward and her hand went under the seat, fishing for the manila envelope. She pulled it forward, fished in the opening and brought out the small white envelope with the negatives in it. She pushed the manila envelope back under the seat and put the smaller envelope inside her shirt. "What's he doing?" she said.

"Tying the dog in," I said. "He'll notice that the negatives are gone."

"Maybe. Maybe not."

I could hear Skinner's voice as he came back toward the open cab door. "That's my cousin and her husband," he said. "We're going over to Reno to win some money."

"If you come back into California, be sure you cross-tie that dog. Next time it's a ticket and that will set you back a hundred dollars."

"Thank you, Officer," Skinner said, sliding in behind the wheel. The cop went back to his car and Skinner pulled out carefully into the traffic.

"Asshole," he said. "Chickenshit. It's the Texas plates. Probably gave him a hard-on to rattle my cage."

We dropped down into the Reno basin, surrounded by
mountains, came off the Interstate at the Downtown
sign, and cruised the main street. Despite the fact that it was
still late afternoon, the lights were on everywhere, a flashing
cascade of neon. Skinner stopped in front of the Silver Legacy,
a high-rise hotel/casino.

"What about this one?" he asked.

"It's big enough to get lost in," Olivia said.

"They don't take my dog, we go someplace else," Skinner
said.

But the clerk at the desk said that yes, they accepted pets,
there would be an extra twenty-five dollar charge per night.

"Shit," Skinner said, "where I come from I could get a
room for both of us for that."

The desk clerk smiled. We stood in the cavernous lobby
with our bags while he punched buttons on a computer. The
noise of the adjoining casino—bells and shouts mixed with
music—washed over us. Nobody seemed to pay attention to
the tall, scruffy man with the dog at his heel. Olivia had been

right. In places like this we were anonymous. We would melt into the rush of gamblers and vacationers, old ladies with cups of quarters and cowboys and young couples, some of them in shorts and flip-flops, women in tank tops and men in suits and ties. Skinner said he wanted adjoining rooms but the clerk said that because of Bandit, his room would be on a different floor. "We set aside rooms for guests with pets," he explained.

Skinner had no baggage, just the manila envelope that he clutched in one hand and a jacket in the other. Olivia used a credit card to pay for the rooms, and it occurred to me that people who could find us at the River Resort would have no trouble finding the location of a credit card use.

I leaned across the counter and said, "Quite frankly, we don't want anyone to know that we're registered here. Together, if you know what I mean," and I leaned my head in Olivia's direction.

"Your room number is secure, sir," he said, his face impassive. "No one will give out the location of your room or the names of the occupants without your permission." 1,200 Rooms, the brochure on the counter said. And Olivia and I wouldn't be here long. We had the negatives and at the first opportunity, Skinner and Bandit were history.

We got as far as the elevators when Olivia suddenly said, "Damn! He didn't give me back my credit card." She handed her bag to Skinner. "Hold this," she said.

Skinner and I watched while she went to the check-in counter, beckoned to the clerk and spoke to him. We waited until she came back, holding her credit card.

Skinner and Bandit were on the sixth floor, Olivia and I on the tenth, but Skinner passed the sixth floor, got off the elevator with us and followed us down to our room. Olivia inserted the plastic key card in the door, the light flashed green and we went inside. Through the window we could see the Sierras, dark blue against the evening sky.

"You're not supposed to be here with your dog," Olivia said.

"They gonna send security up here to take us out?" he said.

"I think not. Right now we got some things to do." He sat next to the window and put the envelope on the table in front of him.

"I got the negatives, you got some way to find out who's in this picture." He opened the envelope and slid out my prints. He pointed to the one of the five men in front of the Quonset hut.

"This here is Ronnie Milsap, next to him is Cindy's brother, and this here is the sergeant. They is all dead. That leaves these two. This here one is Luther Andros." He pointed to the shorter of the two other men. "Cindy says this here is the one who would want them pictures." He pointed to a muscular-looking kid with spikey hair and a cocky grin.

"Is that all there is?" he said. "Nothing more? No other photographs?" He reached back into the envelope and my breath stopped. He felt inside, turned the envelope upside down.

"You fuckers," he said. His voice had not lost its measured cadence, but it was angry. "Where's that little white envelope what was in here?"

"You've lost the negatives," Olivia said.

"I ain't lost them. You took them. Probly while I was tying Bandit up in the back of my truck for that chickenshit cop." He reached inside his shirt and pulled out the gun. He had tucked it inside the waist of his trousers and pulled his shirt over it. I had wondered where it had gone. He laid it on the table.

"You," he said, pointing at me. "Stand up. Take off your clothes." When I hesitated, he rose from his chair. "Don't make me do something I don't particularly want to do."

I bent, took off my shoes and socks, stood and dropped my pants. I unbuttoned my shirt, took it off and then dropped my shorts. I stood, naked in front of him.

"I didn't think you done it," he said. "Now you," and he picked up the gun and pointed it at Olivia.

She unbuttoned her shirt, shrugged out of it and dropped it on the bed. She slipped out of her shoes, bent to slide her jeans down her legs. She stepped out of them. "Satisfied?" she said.

"All of it," he said. "Every fucking stitch."

Olivia unsnapped her bra and tossed it on the bed. Her skin glistened with sweat. The air-conditioned room suddenly felt cold. She slid her panties down and stepped out of them.

"Satisfied now?" she said. There was a thin red line where the knife point had opened her thigh. She stood, defiantly, hands at her sides, and I thought I had never seen anything quite so beautiful, but Skinner seemed to be paying little attention to her remarkable body.

"Turn around, both of you."

We both turned, then faced him.

"Empty your bags." He pointed to the floor.

"You lost the fucking negatives," Olivia repeated. "Or maybe they're down in your truck. Maybe they came out of that envelope under the seat."

He waved the pistol at the floor again. Olivia and I emptied our bags. Mine was an old duffel, hers a small carry-on. We looked at the two piles of clothing on the floor. "Shake everything out," Skinner said. Bandit began to sniff at my dirty socks.

"Now the computer," he said. pointing to Olivia's laptop case. She took it out, opened it up. And we stood, naked, in front of the piles of clothing and toothbrushes and Olivia's cosmetics.

I was astounded. I had watched her slip the envelope inside her shirt. Skinner had been with us every step of the way to the room.

"I suppose I could look to see if you tucked it inside your pussy," he said. "I might have to poke around in there for some time."

He looked at me. "You might of shoved it up your asshole, Mikey, but right now you'd be shitting it out, so that ain't likely." He leaned back in his chair. "You're a clever bitch, ain't you?" he said.

"What's that supposed to mean?" Olivia responded.

"You went back for your credit card. But my guess is you already had your credit card. You give them negatives to the desk clerk and he put them in the hotel safe, didn't he?"

Jesus, I thought, he's a step ahead of me. Skinner waited, still tipped back in the chair. He turned to look out the window. "Nice view," he said. He turned back. "So, bitch, you and me is going back down there and you're going to get them out."

Olivia crossed her arms in front of her breasts. It wasn't a matter of modesty, that I could tell. It was a defiant posture and when she spoke there was no doubt about it. She might just as well have been fully clothed.

"You can go fuck yourself. Nobody gets those negatives out of the hotel safe unless I sign for them, and I'm not about to go down there with you and do that. And you're not about to do anything more than wave that gun at me. You know better than that. I think the expression is, 'big gun, small dick.' Would that be about right?"

"You want to find out which one is bigger?"

"Right now what we all want to find out is who's the man in that photograph who wants the negatives so badly he's willing to kill people for them. And I'm your best bet. So they stay there in that safe, and when we do find out, we go down together and get them and we turn them into more fucking cash than you've ever seen in your pathetic life. And now, if you don't mind, I'm putting my pants back on. It's cold in here." She bent and stepped into her Levis, pulling them up, buttoning them. She slid her arms into the shirt. Skinner watched her carefully.

"You," he said to me. "Put your fucking clothes on. Seems like every time I turn around you're buck nekkid. How much money we talking about?" he asked Olivia.

She buttoned her shirt, pulled her hands through her hair to the back of her head. She twisted her hair into a knot and suddenly she looked very French, her cheekbones sharp and her green eyes wide.

"I don't know," she said. She looked at me. "It's enough to go live on a beach in Mexico and forget about the rest of the world."

"I ain't got no desire to live on a beach in Mexico," Skinner said. "About as much Mex as I can talk is 'how much' and 'I ain't finished.'"

"When we're done you won't have to ask 'how much' anymore," Olivia said. She knelt on the floor to repack the things in her bag.

"How you gonna find out who the dude is?" Skinner asked.

"First things first. You and Bandit go down to the doggy floor and get cleaned up. Buy yourself a clean shirt."

"I ain't leaving you alone. You'll go down there, get them negatives and go off to your Mexican beach house. Don't take me for a fool."

"You and your dog can't stay here."

"I can stay anywhere I goddamn well please."

"No, you can't," Olivia said. "The last thing we need is to draw attention to ourselves, and if you stay here with that dog, we'll have hotel security knocking on the door. The negatives stay in the hotel safe. Michael and I are not going to skip. Luther Andros lives in Illinois, so it's too late to try to contact him now. Tomorrow morning we'll do that. I know who he is."

"So do I," Skinner said. "I looked him up. But how you gonna find the other dude?"

"You leave that to me. You take my laptop with you. That way you'll know I'm still here."

"You could just go and rent another one of them," Skinner said.

"But the one I rent won't have on it what's in mine. And I need that information to make the connection."

Skinner looked doubtful.

"Trust me," Olivia said.

"I wouldn't trust you no further than I could throw you," he said.

Olivia slid her jeans down until the red cut on her thigh showed. She put a finger on it. "I owe you," she said. "There's going to be a scar there that will remind me of what you did last night. Every time I touch it, I'm going to see you stepping through that doorway. And you can take that to the bank."

Skinner smiled and I realized that it was the first time I had seen a genuine smile on his face. "You skip on me and I'll find you. I'll fucking find you and you'll have more than a little scar to remember me by."

After Skinner and Bandit had left, Olivia said, "We still need him. When we make the exchange of the negatives for the money, we need Skinner and his gun. Otherwise we're sitting ducks."

"You think you can find out who the other man is?"

"I know it. Tomorrow morning we do it. Right now we need to get cleaned up and order something from room service, and maybe you'll get lucky." She laughed and peeled off her shirt.

"On second thought," she added, "room service can wait."

Skinner showed up early with Bandit and the laptop. When I opened the door he came in with a cup of coffee in one hand and a bagel in the other, the laptop tucked under his arm. It was obvious that he had showered, but he was still unshaven and wore the same clothes.

"At least you got your fucking pants on," he said. "But my guess is you had 'em off last night and so did she."

Olivia came out of the bathroom, a towel wrapped around her hair, wearing only the white shirt. It came down just below her crotch and Skinner said, "I went through that casino down there this morning but there was no jackpot that looked as rich as that."

Olivia reached up to wrap the towel more tightly around her hair and as she did so, the shirt rose and Skinner let out an explosive. "Damn!" He set the laptop on the small table. "I would tell you to put some pants on, sweetie, but you're built a lot different from Mikey here."

Olivia found her Levis, pulled them on and sat at the table.

"It's seven o'clock here. That means it's nine o'clock where Andros lives. Time to get to work."

She opened the laptop and the keys began to click.

"What are you doing?" I asked.

"Andros will be easy to find. He's the Attorney General for the State of Illinois. But we need more about his buddy before we call him. I've got bank records. The payments to my mother left an electronic trail, and I spent the day before I came up to that cabin with an old boyfriend."

"That must have been quality time for him," Skinner said.

"I got what I wanted," Olivia said. "And you need to put a cork in it, because it's what you want, too."

She continued to click the keys of the laptop. "This will take some time," she said. She looked at me. "You might want to get room service to bring up some breakfast."

I ordered from room service and when breakfast came, Skinner put Bandit in the bathroom. There were eggs and sausage and more coffee and a side order of steak for the dog.

"You didn't make nothing like this for me, Mikey," Skinner said. "I changed my mind. I ain't gonna marry you. I'm gonna marry this fine piece of ass." He waved a piece of toast in Olivia's direction. She ignored him.

It was an hour later when Olivia said, "This is as far as I can go. The money came from a bank in Chico, California. Which means that he lives there or someplace near there. Nobody uses a bank in a town that small unless it's close to them. It went through the bank's clearing house in San Francisco before it ended up in her account."

"You got a name?" Skinner asked.

"Not yet. But with this we can get it out of Andros. Once we get the name, we arrange a meeting. The question is, where can we do this without giving him a chance to ambush us?"

"I know the place," I said. "It's in Oroville, thirty miles south of Chico. It's perfect."

"Where is it?"

"It's a fish hatchery. Right below the Oroville Dam. It's a big hatchery for the salmon run that comes up the Feather River. They had to put it there when they built the dam. It's a perfect spot."

"How perfect?"

"There's a parking lot. It's isolated. There are ramps from that parking lot that go down toward the river, but they loop back into a view chamber. There's a fish ladder that comes up from the river into the hatchery, and they have this concrete bunker with windows inside so tourists can see the salmon when they come up. We park in the lot. That's where we meet them. Skinner stays in his truck, You and I go down into that grotto. Our guy follows. So we're isolated. There's no way they can ambush us, no way anybody can see us or hear us. We do this early in the morning, when there won't be anybody there. It's too early in the season for tourists, anyway. We can make the exchange, and then he comes back up. Skinner tracks him until he gets in his car. He'll have thugs with him, but it won't matter. We don't come up until he leaves."

"You're sure about this?"

"I went there a couple of times. I was doing a photo shoot for a duck club near Oroville. I had time to kill. It's a fucking spooky place, but it's only a half hour from Chico, and once we're down in there, nobody can surprise us."

You're sure?" Olivia said again.

"Nothing. No helicopters, no airplanes, no speeding cars, no long-range rifles. I know it!"

"Okay," she said. "I'll trust you on this. Now we pin the butterfly to the wall. I've got a phone number for Andros in Chicago."

She took out her cell phone and dialed a number. When someone answered, she asked for Luther Andros. There was a pause and she made a thumbs-up sign toward Skinner and me.

"No," she said, "he *will* talk to me. Tell him that I am calling about something that happened in Viet Nam to the Sarge." There was a pause and she repeated it again. "Sarge," she said, and slowly spelled out the name.

"No," she said. "I'll wait. I can guarantee that Mr. Andros will take this call."

She looked at me and smiled. I watched as she raised one hand and absently slipped it inside her shirt, stroking her skin. Then she spoke again.

"Mr. Andros? No, it doesn't matter who I am. Only what I have to say to you."

Another pause.

"My name is not important. What's important is that I have something you want very badly. You and someone else."

Another pause.

"There's one photograph of five men standing, facing the camera. A second one of a man on fire. A third one of a soldier about to shoot a woman and a child. Another of the woman and the child with their faces blown off. And one with the village going up in flames. That satisfy you?"

Apparently he said something and Olivia was silent. She turned to look out the window at the early morning light on the mountains.

"You can repeat that until hell freezes over, Mr. Andros. I'll take your word that you aren't the one who has sent thugs to threaten us. But you know who did. What I want is a number for your buddy. The one who stands next to you in that photograph. Not Ronnie Milsap or Chip Piper. They got their heads bashed in and got dumped in a Texas river. Am I boring you, Mr. Andros? Is this old stuff you'd rather not hear?"

Pause.

"No, I won't say his name. Not over the telephone. You know who he is and I know who he is. And I want a number where I can call him and he can talk to me. And I want you to tell him that I'm going to call. Within minutes. Is that clear?"

Andros spoke again and I could tell that Olivia was interrupting him.

"No, you've got that wrong. It's not hard these days to ferret out a name. He dropped money in the photographer's wife's bank account for ten years. He left an electronic trail. How do you think we found you?"

Another pause.

"You're right. If I have his name, I should know where he is. And I do. But his numbers are all unlisted. And my guess is that you know a number that works."

He spoke again and she interrupted him again. "No, you don't understand. There are other people who want these negatives as well. Your man wants them badly. We're willing to deal, but we're not willing to sit here until he sends some more thugs after us. We've had enough of that."

A pause.

"I know, you say it's not your idea. But you're part of it, Mr. Andros, and you can unravel this ugly garment by giving me a number and making that call. I have nothing more to say."

She paused, then held out the phone to me. "He wants to talk to you."

I put the phone to my ear.

"Is this Michael MacSwain?" the voice asked.

"Yes."

"You're the one who has the negatives?"

"Yes."

"Who is the young woman I spoke to?"

"She has no name."

"Everybody has a name."

"Not this time. Are you clear about what she wants?"

"You have the negatives?"

"Yes."

"Did you make prints?"

"I did, but they're worthless. Anybody could claim they were photo-shopped. The negatives are proof of what happened."

"We didn't know he was taking pictures," the voice said. "The only time we knew he was taking a picture was when he took the photo of the five of us."

"He used a long lens for the others."

Olivia was making motions that I should hang up.

"We'll call you back in ten minutes," I said. and closed the phone. I was sweating and the phone was slippery in my hand.

"What now?" I said.

"We wait, call him back, and if he's in enough of a panic, he'll give us a number for our mystery man. We know our man lives in Chico. Or the Central Valley. And he's a powerful man. We're close to the jackpot, Michael."

Skinner was antsy. He kept pacing the room, stopping to look out the window at the street far below, and when Bandit came close to him, he gave him a soft kick, pushing the dog away.

"You need to take a walk," Olivia said. "Work off some energy. You're making me nervous."

"We're close to finding the motherfucker," he said.

"You smelling the money?" I asked.

"More than that," he said.

"Go on," Olivia said." Nothing is going to happen here until we call Andros back. This will take awhile."

"You sure you'll nail the bastard?" Skinner asked.

"I'm sure," Olivia said. "By this time tomorrow, we'll be looking at him face to face."

Skinner and Bandit left and Olivia took the phone, dialed Andros again. This time the secretary put us through immediately. Olivia turned the volume up on the phone and held it so that I could hear the tiny voice, too.

"You can talk to him," Andros said. "I've got a number where you can reach him. It's not a listed number and it's on a cell."

"Chico," Olivia said. There was a pause.

"You know where he lives?"

"I know where he lives and I know who he is," Olivia said. "We want to do this quickly. Once we call him, you're out of the loop. We'll forget who you are."

"Ben isn't happy about this," he said. "He wants to do this through intermediaries."

"No, we do it with him or we don't do it at all." Olivia had raised her eyebrows at the mention of the name, Ben. "When was the last time you saw him?" she asked.

"Not for a long time. Well, the last time I *saw* him was in yesterday's *New York Times.* Listen: I want nothing more to do with this. I want it to go away."

"And it will," Olivia said. "Give me the number and if he answers, you've heard the last of it. I guarantee that."

Andros gave us a number in the 530 area code.

"And he's expecting me to call?" she asked.

"He said he would wait for the call." The line went dead.

"We need yesterday's *New York Times*," Olivia said. "Go down to the desk. They'll have one someplace. Bring it back up here as soon as you can. The less Skinner knows, the better it is."

"He's nervous about something."

"You said he smells the money. You're right about that. Now go."

I took the elevator to the lobby. There was no sign of Skinner but he could have been anyplace. No doubt he had gone outside so that Bandit could take a leak. The desk clerk went through a door, came back with a newspaper. "Yesterday's *Times*, sir. Anything else I can do for you?"

"Thanks," I said, and laid a five-dollar bill on the counter.

"No charge sir."

"That's for you," I said. "I never got this paper, did I?"

I was paranoid at this point about everything. I took the elevator back to the room, rifling through the paper as I rose to the tenth floor, but I found nothing that would offer a clue to our man. Inside the room Olivia took the paper, laid it on the bed and began to go carefully through it. When she got to the national political page, she said, "Bingo!" She pointed to a photograph of a man standing with the majority leader of the Senate. **Litvak Confirmation Hearings Set**, read the headline. His name was Ben Litvak, and he was the odds-on favorite to be the next Supreme Court Chief Justice. The article noted that he was from California, had strong ties to agribusiness in the Central Valley where he had made a fortune, and was a middle-of-the-road liberal. A lawyer, he was presently a justice on the Ninth Circuit Court of Appeals. He had held that position for ten years.

"Just about the time those checks started arriving," Olivia said. "No wonder those negatives were hot property. It says here he's a decorated Viet Nam veteran, active in humanitarian issues. A picture of him blowing away the heads of a Vietnamese woman and her baby would sure put the brakes on that nomination."

She took the photograph of the soldier aiming his rifle at the woman and child and laid it next to the *New York Times* photo. "It's him," she said. "Forty years older, but it's him."

"And who would be the other people? The other ones who were trying to get those negatives?"

"My guess is that it would be right-wingers who don't want him on the court. Somehow, they heard about the negatives, and you were suddenly the target."

"What now?"

"We give Ben a call. Maybe he'll be happy to hear from us."

She dialed the number. It was answered almost immediately and Olivia said, "This is about some photographic negatives. Is this Ben Litvak?"

He said something, and she said, "I need to know that you're Ben Litvak. Tell me who just called you and tell me the names of the men in your squad in Viet Nam."

Again she waited.

"We have the negatives. You want them. You've gone to considerable lengths to get them. You can have them as early as tomorrow morning if you are willing to pay for them."

"No, that isn't enough."

"Yes, he's here."

She handed the phone to me. The voice asked, "Are you the young photographer who found the negatives?"

"Yes."

"I offered the young lady a hundred thousand dollars for them. I should think that would be enough."

I looked at Olivia. She was holding up five fingers.

"Five hundred thousand," I said.

"Jesus Christ! You're not serious!"

"You sent men to get them. People have suffered."

"That wasn't my intent. I told them to get the negatives and never mind the cost, but things got out of control."

"You're forgetting two dead Viet Nam vets who were fished out of a Texas River."

"And that raises the price?"

Olivia couldn't hear what he was saying, but she was making a thumbs-up sign at what I was saying.

"I can make a wire transfer to a bank of your choice."

"No, we want it in cash and we want it delivered by you."

"Why must it be me?"

"It's either you or the other people who want those negatives. You must know about them."

There was a pause. Then he said, "It will take a day to get that much cash."

"In the morning, day after tomorrow," I said. "Do you know where the salmon hatchery is in Oroville?"

"Yes."

"Six o'clock. In the parking lot of the hatchery. And this will all be over."

"Can't someone else make the exchange?"

"We know what you look like, Ben. Nice photograph of you in the *Times*. Nobody else."

I hung up.

"Fucking brilliant," Olivia said, throwing her arms around me. "Mexico, here we come!"

At that moment, there was a knock at the door. We both fell silent, and then heard Skinner's voice. "It's me."

Olivia opened the door.

"You gonna call him?" he said.

"We did. Day after tomorrow and we're rich."

"How much?"

"Thirty-three thousand for each of us. He'll pay a hundred grand. We need to order a bottle of champagne, Michael. It's time to celebrate!"

She had just cheated Skinner out of a hundred and thirty thousand dollars. I wondered if I would get my full share. And I wondered if the invitation to Mexico would include an address. Or would I, like Skinner, be left holding a bag that had been emptied out.

"Fucking-A," Skinner said, "that sure beats a poke in the eye with a sharp stick."

It was five hours through the Sierras to the Central Valley and up to Oroville. Skinner's old truck climbed the interstate over Donner Pass, a spit of rain showing on the windshield, and then we dropped down into Grass Valley. From there it was a long winding slide out of the foothills into Marysville. In the middle of the night there was little traffic, mostly 18-wheelers, and we said very little. Olivia dozed, her head against the window on the passenger side. I was crammed in the middle and Bandit was at our feet. Our bags in the back were covered with an old tarp that flapped in the wind. At Marysville we turned north and, in the first light that grew over the Sierras to our right, I could see rice fields that had been harvested. There were flat fields of stubble with patches of water here and there, and egrets along the side of the road lifted off as we approached, tucking their heads into an S, rowing through the air with measured wingbeats away from us. We turned off the highway at Oroville, drove through the town. There were empty store fronts along the main street. It was a town that had seen better days. We crossed the Feather River just below the dam and took the turnoff that announced HATCHERY.

I had remembered it the way it was: an empty parking lot that overlooked the river with the hatchery on the bluff above it. There were rocky ledges along the edge of the river, and the water spilled over the smaller dam that blocked the salmon run. A fish ladder rose from the base of the dam, and I could see black shapes of salmon thrashing around, some of them making a charge at the first cascading step of the fish ladder.

Skinner pulled into the parking lot and backed his truck into a slot so that he would have an unobstructed view of the other parking spaces. It was five-thirty and there was enough light so that we could clearly see the entire parking lot, the entrance off the highway, and the river below, churning over the rocks. Skinner got out, Bandit followed him, and he went down the ramp toward the viewing grotto. He came back a few minutes later. Bandit jumped into the back of the truck and Skinner slid in behind the wheel.

"It's empty," he said. "Nobody waiting to surprise you."

We waited. Skinner finally got out and let Bandit run after birds along the edge of the asphalt.

The black SUV turned into the parking lot entrance and Skinner came back to the truck.

"Show time," he said, sliding in again behind the wheel. It was an expensive SUV—large, shiny—and it came to a stop facing us twenty yards away. The lights blinked once. We waited. Finally a back door opened and a man stepped out. He was wearing a three-quarter-length leather coat, glasses, and dark slacks. His hands were thrust deep into the coat pockets. Skinner opened the door just enough to stand on the running board and shouted, "Hands out of your pockets!"

The man lifted his hands out of his pockets and began to walk toward us. Skinner aimed his pistol at the man, bracing it on the door of the truck so that the occupants of the other vehicle could see what he was doing.

"Right there!" he yelled. The man stopped. The passenger door of the SUV opened, and we could see a man with a gun doing exactly what Skinner was doing. His gun was pointed at Skinner and the truck.

"Time you two took a hike," Skinner said, turning to me. "They know that if they do anything, I got him in my sights. Let's hope he's our man and not some poor fucker they sent out as a decoy."

Olivia opened the door and slid out. I followed her. We turned and started for the pathway that led down to the viewing chamber. Within seconds we were behind the concrete ledge that framed the path. We turned again at the bottom and went toward the opening. It was a dark tunnel, wet, with puddles of water, and it smelled dank. There was no light inside. Along one wall were several long windows and behind them gray sunlight penetrated the water that surged on the other side of the glass. There was a hollow rushing sound and the watery chambers had no fish in them, only bubbles spinning through the coursing water. Each chamber was a separate pool, with a waterfall at the upper end. The fish would have to gather speed in the pool, perhaps ten yards long, and leap into the next, higher, pool. It was all framed in concrete, thick, like military gun emplacements or the foundations of skyscrapers.

A salmon came into view, a huge, slab-sided fish, scars on its skin, its great unblinking eye looking through the glass at us It was the size of a boy's leg. Perhaps, I imagined, it was examining us. Or, more likely, we were invisible to this creature that had come three hundred miles from the sea.

We waited.

We heard the click of footsteps, expensive men's shoes with leather heels, and the black outline of a figure appeared in the opening. By the time he had come to the window, we recognized him. It was the same face we had seen in the *New York Times.*

"You're Ben Litvak," I said.

"And you must be the little asshole photographer who's caused all this trouble."

"I think the trouble was caused a long time ago," I said. "And I think you caused it."

"Who's this?" he said, turning to Olivia.

"You put me through college, Mr. Litvak."

"And this is the gratitude I get for doing that?"

His hair was close-cropped, tinged with gray, and he had the look of a man who was used to being listened to. He carried a leather attaché case. On his wrist was an expensive watch that shone briefly in the reflected light from the window of the fish ladder. The salmon was still there, just behind his head. The eye was brown and silver and the tail moved slowly as the fish held its position in the rushing water. Suddenly it throbbed, making a dash toward the cascading upper lip, abruptly turned and came back to the bottom of the pool, where it turned and once again was suspended parallel to the window. With any luck it would reach the top of the ladder where technicians would strip it of its eggs and it would be discarded, its life cycle over.

I wondered if Olivia and I had come to the opposite side of the glass only to be stripped of our eggs and discarded. If anything happened to Skinner, above us in the parking lot, we would not be able to hear the shots.

Litvak held out the case. "Where are the negatives?" he said. Olivia offered the small white envelope as she took the case from him. He turned and, taking out the negatives, one at a time, held them up to the glass. The salmon did not move. It was as if the salmon, too, was examining the images that were illuminated by the dim light.

"What's this one?" he said. He held it out and I looked at it.

"Ronnie Milsap and Chip Piper were dragged out of that river. It was Aaron Sturgis' way of saying, here's where murder was done."

"And this is his wife?"

"Was," I said. "He's dead now, but you know that." He pressed the negative against the glass and looked intently at it.

"Good looking, isn't she?" I said.

"That was a long time ago."

"She's still a beautiful woman."

He turned to Olivia. "Do you take after your mother?"

"Only in the way I look."

"I paid her all those years. Now I'm paying you. I fail to see the difference."

"We're done here," Olivia said. Her voice had a hard edge to it. "You can go back up and get in your expensive car with your gun-toting thugs and go to hell, for all I care."

Olivia and I waited at the concrete ledge at the top of the path until the black SUV had turned onto the highway. At the truck, Skinner was literally bouncing in the seat.

"We got the money!" he said. "Show it to me."

"No," Olivia said. "We need to get out of here as quickly as possible." She shoved the attaché case behind the seat as she got in. "We need to go back to the resort, change the tires on those two cars and get them out of there. We'll divide things up when we do that. And then we take the money and run."

Skinner turned to me. "How do we get from here to there?"

"Go back through town. We take Highway 70, the one that goes up the Feather River Canyon. Maybe an hour and a half and we're there."

"God *damn*!" Skinner shouted, and started the truck.

It was mid-morning when we got to the gate at the bridge. The lock was as we had left it. I had discarded the cut-off portion of chain so that it seemed just as it had been when I had first arrived. At the cabin the two cars were still there, a front tire on each one flat against the ground.

"You two change the tires," Olivia said. "I'm going inside and I'll divide up the money." She was rummaging in my bag in the back of Skinner's truck and she emerged with the unfinished bottle of scotch. "And then we'll celebrate," she said. She went inside the cabin and Skinner and I set about putting on the spare tires. There was no sign that anyone had been at the cabin since we had left it.

Once the tires were changed, Skinner and I went inside the cabin. Bandit curled up on the porch in front of the door.

On the table in the kitchen were three piles of money, three glasses, and the bottle of scotch.

"Here it is." Olivia pointed to one pile. "All yours," she said to Skinner. He picked up the stack. They were crisp one-hundred-dollar bills. "Three hundred and thirty of them," she said.

What I noticed was that the attaché case was nowhere to be seen. In the refrigerator? In one of the kitchen cupboards? But Skinner paid no attention to that. He fingered the bills, fanning out the stack, and then he folded it and stuffed it into his pants pocket.

"Been nice knowing you folks," he said. "Me and Bandit are going back where we belong." He looked at Olivia carefully. Then he said, "You could not of done it without me. I saved your bacon. By rights I ought to get more than a third of this. Without me you would both be dead. And you. little lady, would have had some things done to you that would of made you glad you was about to die. I ain't sure what Mikey done that makes him a full third. He done nothing but find them negatives."

"And without the negatives, you would not have thirty-three thousand dollars stuffed into your pocket," Olivia said. "Don't get greedy, Skinner."

"Ain't much you could do if I did," he said.

Oh no, I thought. He'll take our share and drive off to Texas with it, but I realized that what lay on the table wasn't our share. It was a fraction of our share.

Skinner laughed. "But I ain't a greedy man." Bandit got up and trotted toward the truck when Skinner opened the door. Skinner threw our bags out of the back, started the truck and we watched as it disappeared down the narrow road through the trees.

"What now?" I said.

"You go back to your house, close it out, and you meet me here." She handed me a photograph of a house on a beach. It was a small cottage with a white-washed exterior, and a thatched roof over a lean-to side that was in the shade. The sea was in the right-hand corner of the photo, a rich turquoise blue. I turned the photograph over. On the back was written *Puerto Angel.*

"Where's this?" I asked.

"Below Acapulco. On the Pacific side."

"And you'll be there?" I asked.

"You can put money on it." she said. "Speaking of which." She opened the refrigerator, reached into the freezer compartment, and, using both hands, took out a stack of bills. "Gives new meaning to the words cold cash, doesn't it?" she said. She set the pile on the table on top of the two stacks of bills already there. "We can't put it all in one bank. They raise a red flag when more than ten thousand is deposited in an account. Which means you'd have to find twenty-three banks for your share.. So you'll have to hang onto a chunk of it. When you get to Mexico, they don't have rules like that. Put a hundred thousand into banks here, and bring the rest with you."

She turned back to the table. "We should drink to that." She paused and then said, "Shit! Skinner took the bottle. I didn't see him do that!"

I reached out for the stack of bills, but she put her hand on mine. "No," she said. "We're not in that big of a hurry." There's other ways to celebrate this, and she began to unbutton that white shirt.

Skinner's truck was in my driveway. The front door was open and when I stepped into the room I saw him, sitting at the kitchen table with a six-pack of beer, some tortilla chips and a bowl of salsa.

"What are you doing here?" I said. I had a sinking feeling that Skinner would be a continuing part of my life. Bandit was at his feet and growled as I came to the kitchen door.

"She fucked me over, didn't she?" he said.

"What do you mean?"

"She got more money than she said. I could smell it. And she gave me less than a third of it. She went in that cabin and she pretended that was all there was, but my mother didn't raise no stupid boy. I fucking saved her life. Yours, too. You watch your back, Mikey. She'll fuck you over, too."

Oh shit, I thought, he wants more money. I waited for him to say something but he was silent. He raised the beer can, drained it, crushed the empty can in his hand, and popped another one. "You want a beer?" he asked. I shook my head. There was something about Skinner that was different. His voice still had that measured cadence, as if he weren't all there, but now he seemed casual about what was true. He knew what Olivia had done. But he wasn't doing anything about it, and that was puzzling.

"What makes you think she cheated you?" I asked.

"The fucker who paid up had too much to lose to sell out that cheap. He paid her old lady all those years." Skinner fanned out the bills on the table. "It's a fucking lot of money, anyway. Thirty grand. But it don't matter."

"The money doesn't matter?"

"I got something else. I got the name of the fucker who did it and I know what he looks like."

"Why would you care who killed that Vietnamese woman and child. What difference would it make to you if a village was torched fifty years ago."

"That don't make no difference to me. Only you got it wrong. They told you a pack of lies. You thought it was all about them doing some war crime and that was why they paid you to hand over them negatives. Only that wasn't it at all."

He squatted and Bandit came to him, pressing his muzzle into Skinner's leg, pushing at him, and Skinner pulled at the dog's ears, reached down and stroked the leg. There was something satisfying in what he was doing. Skinner was no longer interested in me or Olivia or the money. He had distanced himself from us.

"What was it you got?" I asked.

"The last guy in the photo, the one of the five guys in front of their hut. You remember showing it to Cindy?"

"Sure." I remembered standing in the scorching heat at the chain link fence while the dogs tumbled at it and Skinner stood impassively with his pistol pointed at me.

"You remember which one Cindy called Sarge?"

"The last one. He looked older than the others."

"He's the one."

"What about him?"

"That was my old man."

"You mean it was your father?"

"My mother was pregnant when he went off to 'Nam. They wasn't married. I never saw him. Until I saw that photograph and Cindy said that was Sarge."

His face as impassive as he mouthed the words, but there was a tension in his voice that was urgent.

"How did you know that was him?"

"Ronnie Milsap. After Chip got killed, Ronnie talked about it. Mostly he was drunk or stoned, but he talked about something that happened in 'Nam that was terrible and he told me my daddy was there. And my daddy got burned alive and one of the guys in his outfit was responsible. He said they called it fragging. You know, when soldiers kill an officer because they don't like him. Ronnie said that my Daddy was gung ho, always wanted to be on point; he was a risk-taker. And two of the guys in the squad were chickenshit and my daddy was all over them. He said they was pussies and not worth snot. Ronnie said him and Chip was scared all the time, but they did what Sarge told them to do. But the other two, all they wanted to do was be where it was safe and nobody was going to shoot at them. So one of them set him up. He paid some gook woman to set a gasoline trap, and when my daddy come out of that hut on fire, that bastard shot him and then he shot that woman what set the trap, and then he shot her child, and he made Ronnie and Chip and that other dude shoot her, too, and they called in a napalm strike and burned the whole fucking place up, including my daddy. So there wasn't no witnesses left to tell what they done. But there was a combat photographer there and he took some pictures. They never knew he took them until later. So all my life I been haunted by my missing daddy, and then I found out that he wasn't just killed over there by the enemy. His own men killed him. And the sumbitch who did in my daddy was still alive and there was these pictures that showed who the sumbitch was. And Olivia's mama lived off the money that her old man squeezed out of the fucker.

"Ronnie said him and Chip didn't want nothing to do with killing the Sarge, but they was caught up in it and they was only eighteen years old and scared shitless. And then they all got medals and nobody knew what happened except them four what was left. But Ronnie said it burned in Chip. It ate away at him, and he was going to go to somebody and spill the beans, and then he ended up in that river. And Ronnie, who you could hardly understand even when he was sober, said he was going to tell somebody and he ended up in that river, too. So I knew that whoever it was still had his fingers in the pie. I run onto Ronnie in Fort Worth, and when this whole thing come up, I went and found Cindy. We ain't married, you know."

"And she knows all of this?"

"She don't know nothing. I never told her. And then you showed up with that photograph. There they was, all five of them—Ronnie and Chip and my old man and Luther and the other asshole, which was the one who planned the whole thing. He was the one what hired the gook lady to set fire to my daddy. He was the one what shot him and he was the one what called in the air strike. Ronnie said he was a smart sumbitch. He went to some fancy-ass law school and then he got drafted and he couldn't get out of it. He was pissed off that he was in 'Nam and he was especially pissed off that my daddy might get him killed."

"But I didn't know how to find him. So I drafted onto the two of you, let you suck me along. And you had them other pictures. The one of my daddy on fire. When I seen that, I knew what I was going to do. The money was of no interest to me. Only finding that sumbitch. And now I know who he is. I seen him and I know how to find him again."

"What are you going to do?" I asked.

"I think maybe I should set the motherfucker on fire. You think that might be the right thing to do?" He said it the way you might say, 'Maybe I should buy some more beer for the party. What do you think?'

"You'll never get close enough to him to do it. Why didn't you shoot him when we saw him at the money exchange?"

"Because none of us would of got out of there alive. That black SUV had his goons in it, and you can bet they had the heat on us. No, I got something better planned."

"You'll never get that close to him again."

"Don't not bet on that, Mikey. I got this far. I ain't gonna quit now. But I need somebody to give me a hand. And that somebody is you, Mikey."

"No. I want no part of it."

He continued to scratch Bandit's ears. "I could sic this dog on you and he would turn and rip your arm off. You know that, don't you?"

"Why would you do that?"

"I might just do it to give him a little exercise. You're in this whole thing up to your belly button, and I could rat you out and you wouldn't get out of the slammer until you are a skinny old man. You can go to Mexico with that clever bitch and fuck her brains out or you can give me a hand. Then you can go to Mexico. Nothing dangerous. You don't have to do nothing except take care of a few details. I need a front man, Mikey.

Somebody who looks presentable and don't scare people off. And that's what you are. If you was to order a burrito in Fort Worth and they was to ask if you wanted hot salsa or mild, you would be the stuff what has no bite, but looks like the other stuff. You are exactly what I need, Mikey."

"And if I won't do this?"

"Then I spill my guts. I show them where there's two bodies in a river and how you helped me to hide them and how you went to Texas to show Cindy some pictures and how you were up to your ass in blackmailing, and I bring the motherfucker down with us, only we all go down together. But I would rather set him on fire and send you off to fuck that gorgeous piece of ass on some beach where you can live like a fucking prince. Seems like a no-brainer to me."

He looked down at the dog. "Bandit, how would you like to bite off Mikey's dick? Be sort of like one of them doggie chew toys."

Bandit raised his head and looked at Skinner as if he were waiting for more direction.

"What do I have to do?" I asked.

"You met Olivia's mama?"

"Yes."

"That picture of her with them negatives. She was a looker, too, like Olivia. She still a good looker?"

"Yes. She still is."

"If she was to find out who it was that sent her all that money, do you suppose she would take a shine to him, maybe try to up the ante?"

"Without the negatives she wouldn't have any leverage."

"She's got a whole lot of deposits to her bank account. Be hard to explain those. And like you said, she's a looker."

"Are you suggesting that she come on to him?"

"It's fucking amazing what can happen when somebody forgets what he's doing while his zipper is undone."

"What makes you think Litvak would get involved with her?"

"His wife is dead, his kiddies are all grown up, he's a good looker, and he's got money. Men like that think they're hot shit. Some good-looking woman drops the hint that she would drop her drawers for him, and it's like leaving out honey for a fly. And she's a loose end. She promises to turn everything over to him, and maybe hints he could get a roll in the hay with her, I think he would take the bait." Skinner fanned the bills back into a stack. "Attractive woman his age. If she's anything like her daughter. . . ." He left the sentence hanging. "In any case, it don't matter. She don't have to fuck him. All she has to do is get him to show up to collect what she says she has."

He fingered the bills into a neat stack, then fanned them out again.

"I give her this and she thinks it's from him. He don't know that. He thinks she's on the make for some cash. But he's not about to give it to her. He might promise something, but it's the end of the line as far as he's concerned."

"How can you be so sure about all this?"

"I ain't so sure. If this don't work, then I got another plan."

"How did you find out about Olivia's mother?"

"While the two of you was up in that hotel room finding out who he was, I was doing a bit of finding out, too. When I went into your bag to get them negatives, I took this." He held up my photo log. In it were names, addresses, notes. And there were notes about Emma, her photograph, her husband, his camera, and the negatives.

Skinner laid the little black book on the table next to the money. "So I know she's still around and I know where she lives. And you would be the key what opens the lock."

"But she doesn't have bank records. She doesn't have anything to hold out to him."

"He don't know that. Suppose somebody tells him that she's got all these bank records and photographs made from them negatives. He gonna just say forget it, or is he going to make sure there ain't no loose ends?

"What would I do?"

"All you have to do is talk to her, Michael. You don't have to do nothing else."

It was the first time he had used my whole name. I was no longer pussy-boy or Mikey. I was somebody he needed to suture a long-open wound. He continued to scratch Bandit's ears and the dog had rested its muzzle on his thigh.

"That dog would do anything for you," I said.

"That's right."

"Would he talk Emma Sturgis into helping you kill Ben Litvak?"

"If he could talk, he would do it."

"I'm not your dog, Skinner."

"No. I ain't gonna scratch you behind the ears. But I think you know where justice lies. And I think you will do the right thing."

And I would be part of a conspiracy to kill a man. Granted, it was a man who had no compunctions about sending killers after me, and a man who had done a terrible thing and had covered it up for years. Nevertheless, I would be conspiring with Skinner to kill him. I had already extorted a huge sum of money. And he was a man who, if left alone, would become the Chief Justice of the United States Supreme Court. It occurred to me that I could rationalize my actions by pretending I was doing a public service. Which, of course, was bullshit. Skinner was going to kill him. He wanted me to help him do it. I wasn't just helping to bury some bodies. This time I was being asked to help pull the trigger.

"I ain't asking you to light the match, Michael," Skinner said. "This here is my unfinished business. Not yours. All you have to do is unlock the door for me. After that, you take your money and you go on down to wherever she is and forget you ever saw me."

"What do you want me to tell Emma?" I said.

"You tell her that you give up those negatives to him. And now he wants to meet up with her, clear things up. Make it right. You call him. I leave it up to you what you tell him. You ain't no dummy, Michael. You'll think up a good story. That's all you have to do. Nothing more." He peeled off five of the hundred dollar bills, and left the others fanned out on the table. "You got any doubts," he added. "You take another look at that picture of my daddy on fire."

He said he needed a day. I could pack up my stuff while he sorted things out and he would be back.

"I ain't got no place to stay," he said, "so I guess I can stay here on your couch."

He stuffed the five hundred dollars in his pocket and left. I spent the rest of the day filling my car with my belongings and driving down to Goodwill. I gave them my darkroom equipment, most of my clothes, the dishes and pans from the kitchen. By five o'clock the house looked empty. I called Mrs. Mortenson and told her I was moving out. I would pay the next month's rent and leave my furniture. She could keep it or have the Salvation Army haul it away.

"Something urgent has come up," I said. I apologized for the abruptness of my move. I ordered a pizza from Ghiringhelli's and a kid delivered it a half hour later. Skinner showed up in time to finish it off. He had two more six-packs of beer and a bottle of Johnny Walker Black Label scotch.

"Here," he said, holding out the bottle. ""Don't let nobody say I drunk your booze and never bought you a drink."

His plan was simple. I was to contact Emma the next day. Let her know that I had found the man who wanted the negatives and had returned them. And that he was anxious to make sure there was no record of his having paid someone all those years. She would meet him in San Rafael. She would promise to close the account and the following day they would meet at a motel in Mill Valley where she would give him the records. And she would give him the prints I had made from the negatives. In exchange she would get some money. Almost thirty thousand dollars.

"Then what happens?" I asked.

"You don't want to know. You make sure she gets him to that motel. She don't have to go there herself. Just promise to meet him there. She ought to give him the hope that there's more in it for him than just a handshake. When he sees that the woman he's been paying for all these years is a looker, fucking her might just be the icing on the cake for him. Wham, bam, thank you ma'am."

I spent the following morning opening bank accounts: Bank of America, Wells Fargo, Bank of California, Bank of Marin, Redwood Credit Union, all of them within twenty minutes of each other. By noon I had gotten rid of a hundred thousand dollars. Then I called Emma Sturgis.

"The photographer, remember?"

"How could I forget you?"

"I have some good news."

"Which is?"

"I located the man who wanted those negatives. He has them now. But there's something else he wants, and you may be interested."

"And what would that be?"

"He deposited money in your bank account. I have some prints that were made from those negatives. He's willing to pay you a considerable sum of money if you'll close that bank account, give him any records or receipts you have, and give him the prints. I hinted that your husband made the prints. I figured I owed it to you."

"Did he give you some money?"

"No. What he did was promise to leave me alone. I don't know how he's involved with those negatives, but he would like to meet you."

"If he's willing to pay me for some cancelled checks, my guess is he's paid you something, too," she said. Her voice had an acerbic edge to it.

"He paid for the damage to my house and my own missing negatives and enough extra to make it worth my while to forget about him and those negatives your husband took."

"So you remember whose negatives they were?"

"I haven't forgotten."

"It sounds like you'll come out of this with a little something." Her voice dripped with sarcasm.

"Yes."

"And now I'm to get my share?"

"Yes to that, too."

"I deserve it," Emma said.

So I went by Emma's place on the Larkspur Boardwalk and it was the same—elegant white walls, slender Giacometti statues, and Emma, who was resplendent in a crimson blouse and white linen pants. I explained to her what would happen. All she had to do was meet him at the restaurant in San Rafael. Tell him what she had. I showed her the prints, but I left out the one that showed the Vietnamese woman and her child with their faces shot off. She would have to go to the bank and close the account and have evidence for him that the account was closed. She could show that to him. She would show him one of the prints. The other records and the rest of the prints she would give to him at a pre-arranged meeting place the following day.

"What's he like?" she asked.

"He's a good looking man about your age, and he's rich and he's powerful."

She brightened at that.

"All you have to do," I said, "Is make sure he comes to the meeting place on time. I'll take care of the rest."

"What about the money?"

"Don't worry. You'll get it."

"How much?"

"Nearly thirty thousand dollars. In cash."

She gave a quick gasp.

The following morning I called Ben Litvak. I got a secretary who asked who I was and I told her to tell him that the photographer was calling. That there was a loose end he would want to tie up. "Tell him it's about Emma Sturgis," I said.

In a few moments he was on the line.

"I thought we were finished," he said. "I wasn't ever going to hear from you again."

"One little thing," I said. "All those payments to Emma Sturgis? They leave a paper trail to you."

"Bullshit. She's got nothing. Electronic transfers. There's no way I can be connected to them."

"But her daughter used them to track you down. If you want to close this out, I can fix it."

"More money."

"No. All you have to do is meet with her. She'll close the account, give you her records. She gets a token payment from me."

"Why would you do that? You want something from me."

"Let's say we want things as neat as you do. I don't want somebody showing up waving a gun at her, because she's connected to her daughter and her daughter is connected to me."

"That wouldn't happen."

"Not on your end. But you need to remember that there are other people who were interested in those negatives, and right now she's got no reason to think she couldn't sell what she has to someone who offered her some cash. She no longer has your monthly deposits."

"It wouldn't matter. I have the negatives. End of discussion."

"There's something else," I said. He was silent. I could hear the faint sound of a siren on the street where he was. He wasn't inside a building. He had taken his cell phone out where no one else could hear him.

"What if her husband made some prints from those negatives and she has those?" I said.

It wasn't exactly a lie. It was a question, but it was enough. "If she has records of bank deposits from you?" I continued. "Somebody could connect those bank deposits and those photographs and it would be enough to fuck you over. And if things go bad for you, then things go bad for us. Olivia and I want everything finished. As much as you do."

"I don't like this."

"Nobody likes any part of this. Not you, not me, not Olivia, not anybody. It's bad news all the way. All you have to do is have a glass of wine with her and be your charming self. She wants to see you, face to face. She thinks you're going to give her some money. You don't have to. I'll take care of that."

"Why would you do that?"

"I need to convince you that we're not after anything else. That all we want is for this to come to a quiet end."

"What does she know about the negatives?"

"That they were obviously important to you. She thinks I gave them to you."

"But she knows what they showed?"

"She has the prints. I'm not sure she understands the significance of them. It's a bunch of soldiers. You can deduce from them that bad things happened. For all she knows, you're protecting someone else."

"And where do I meet her?"

"In San Rafael. At a restaurant called Il Davide on A Street. There are tables outside on the sidewalk. She'll be at one of them."

"When?"

"Tomorrow would be good. You leave Chico by ten o'clock, you'll be in San Rafael before one."

"I'm supposed to be in Washington tomorrow."

"Change your plans. This needs to be done now."

"And this is the end of it?"

"By Friday I won't even be in this country."

Emma's meeting with Ben Litvak went off without a hitch. I parked my car in the bank parking lot opposite the restaurant where I could see her sitting at the table. He came out of the parking lot garage, followed discreetly by two men who sat at another table. I watched as she spoke and she bent forward, apparently listening to what he was saying. She laughed and reached into her purse, a large leather bag on the empty chair next to her, taking out one of the photographs and a sheet of paper. It was the photo of the five men and the paper would be the evidence that she had closed her account. I watched as she explained that she had the rest of the prints and the bank records in a safe place and that she would meet him at a motel in Mill Valley the following afternoon at two o'clock. We had rehearsed what she would say, and she had been a quick study. Several times she reached up to stroke her hair back from her face, and the familiar hand went inside the blouse, touching her chest, absently stroking herself. She's good, I thought. I could believe her myself. I had told Litvak that she would ask for some money, and he was to promise that she would get it, and that I would be the delivery boy. The waiter came with two glasses of champagne. Classy touch, I thought. And I knew how that had happened. He had asked what she would like and she had said, 'Champagne, of course.' Their glasses touched and they chatted for a few more minutes before he rose. He took her hand, held it a moment, and as he stepped toward the parking garage, the two other men left their cups of coffee to follow him. He doesn't go anywhere without them, I thought. Were they Secret Service? Private rent-a-cops? Bodyguards? As a Supreme Court Chief Justice nominee, did he rate that kind of protection? Eventually Emma rose and crossed the street to where I was parked. She got into the car and said, "He's a fascinating man. He remembered Aaron. I'm looking forward to tomorrow."

"No," I said. "You won't be there tomorrow. The photographs and the bank records will be in that motel room. It's going to be unlocked and he's going to go into it and get them. But you won't be there." She looked crestfallen.

"Why not?"

"You didn't see the two men in dark suits who sat at a table at the other end."

"I saw them. What of them?"

"They're always with him. He's a dangerous man, Emma. I have the money. When he picks up the photographs and the papers, I give you the cash. And you and I are done with this mess that your husband left us in."

"So what was today all about? Was I just the bait on the hook?"

"A bit of that. But very attractive bait."

"Apparently not attractive enough," she said. "I would appreciate it if you would drive me home."

I did not go to the motel the next afternoon. Skinner had told me that I should wait until noon, and if he had not called me, to give Emma the money and then take off. At noon there had been no call, so I drove by her house and gave her the envelope, fat with hundred-dollar bills. She opened it, but didn't count them.

"You're an interesting young man, Michael," she said. "You should have met me thirty years ago. But of course, you were a child then, weren't you?" Her voice had a familiar hard edge to it and then I remembered Olivia saying, "Fuck you, Skinner," using that same razor-sharp tone as she stood naked, facing him with her arms folded across her breasts.

I drove to Santa Rosa where an auto recycler gave me $400 for my car. It would be taken apart and sold, piece by piece. They gave me a ride to the Santa Rosa Airporter depot where I got on the bus for the San Francisco airport. By that evening I was in Dallas, waiting for a flight to Mexico. With several hours to kill, I sat in the bar and nursed a drink, half-heartedly watching the television that was attached to the wall in one corner Suddenly I saw something familiar and I asked the bartended to turn up the volume. There on the screen was the parking lot of the motel in Mill Valley. There were fire trucks and police cars and a reporter who was describing how Supreme Court nominee Ben Litvak had been brutally attacked. He had been set on fire in one of the motel rooms and had stumbled out of the room toward a car where two security agents were waiting for him. He had burns over ninety percent of his body and was not expected to live. Whoever had doused him with gasoline and set him on fire had shot him in the back as he staggered, screaming, from the motel door. The assailant had escaped through a back door of the blazing unit. Police had interviewed the motel owner who said the room had been rented by a man with a southern accent who drove an old truck with California license plates. According to the Mill Valley police, the plates had been stolen.

And then the newscast switched to the weather. Tropical storms had slowed air traffic. Flights into and out of Mexico were expected to resume that evening.

The plane landed at Acapulco and I looked for some way to get to Puerto Angel. I finally found a cab that would take me there. We rocketed out of the city, following the bumpy highway that went south.

"*Un hora, señor,*" said the cabbie. An hour. When we reached the town he asked where I wanted to be dropped off.

"In the square," I said. "*La Plaza.*" It was mid-afternoon and there was no evidence of anyone in sight. A stray dog loped into the square and headed toward me. Always there's a dog I thought It stopped a few yards off and decided that I wasn't worth further investigation.

I went into the cantina and it, too, was empty. The bartender was polishing glasses, and when I leaned across the bar he turned to me, still holding a glass.

"Can you tell me where Señora Sturgis lives?" I asked.

"*No lo comprendo,*" he said.

"Señora Sturgis." How could I describe her, I thought. "*Bonita.*" I said. I mimed the shape of her body with my hands. "*Americana.*"

His face broke into a smile. "*Si, la bonita Americana,*" he said. He pointed toward the sea that glittered at the end of the street, then made a gesture to his left. "*La ultima casa,*" he said

"*Gracias,*" I replied. I walked out into the hot sun. The sea was no more than a hundred yards from the plaza. When I got to the beach, I turned left, and walked along the edge of the wet, packed sand until I came to a half dozen isolated small cottages. The last one was a duplicate of the one in the photograph she had given me.

The interior was dark and at first I did not see her. I heard her voice: "Michael!" and then I saw her on the bed, her smooth legs pale white in the darkness.

"It's siesta time," she said." You must be the only one walking about in this heat."

"Apparently," I said.

"But you found me."

"The bartender in the cantina called you '*la Bonita Americana.*'"

She laughed "Take off your clothes," she said. "Come and sleep with me."

But we didn't sleep. We kissed. Her mouth was open and it was as if she had not eaten for a long time, was ravenous, and her lips and tongue and teeth searched me for sustenance, sucking and biting at me, looking for something, anything, to fill her mouth, and then we made love and she was ravenous all over again, only this time it was her whole body that took me in. Her body became slick with sweat, as slippery as a fish. Then she was silent, lying on her back next to me and when I said, "You okay?" she replied, "My whole body is a beating heart. I am all pulse, filled with blood."

She closed her eyes and within seconds her breathing was even. I touched the side of my head to her chest, pressing my ear to her skin, listening to the beat of her heart. It was a delicate drum, slow and measured. It was nearly an hour before I fell asleep, exhausted. When I woke she was standing next to the bed, holding a cold beer. The condensation dripped from it and she reached down and touched it to my belly.

"Is this permanent?" I asked.

"Nothing in life is permanent, Michael. Life itself isn't permanent. A month, a year. I have no idea. Right now. That's all that's important."

"There's something else," I said.

"What would that be?"

"Ben Litvak is dead."

She lifted the beer bottle, and pressed it to her cheek. "How?" she asked.

"When?"

"Yesterday. Skinner set him on fire."

"Jesus," she said. "Skinner did what?"

"He set him on fire. And then shot him."

"But Skinner went back to Texas!"

"No, he didn't. When I got home, he was there. The soldier that was on fire in those photographs? That was his father. And Litvak was the one who paid a Vietnamese woman to set him

on fire. And then Litvak shot Skinner's father. And then he shot
the Vietnamese woman and her child."

"Why?"

"It's a long story. It's done. That's all that matters. Skinner
got his revenge. That's what he wanted all along."

"How did he do it?"

"He arranged a meeting with Litvak. Actually, I was the
one who arranged it." I stopped. There seemed no point in telling Olivia of her mother's involvement.

"Where did this happen?" she asked.

"At a motel in Mill Valley, just north of San Francisco. Litvak went inside, came out on fire, and then Skinner shot him.
But in the flames and smoke, nobody saw Skinner.

"Skinner knew you cheated him on the money, but he said
he didn't care. All he wanted was to find out who torched his
father, and when he found it was Litvak, he closed the circle."

"And you arranged the meeting? Why?"

"I'm not sure. Somehow it seemed the right thing to do."

"What happened to Skinner?"

"I suppose he's back in Texas. With his dog. I doubt if he
will lose any sleep over it."

"And you?"

"I'm here. With you."

She stood at the edge of the bed and I remembered something I had seen in the museum in San Francisco. In a small
gallery that looked out over the trees there was a statue of a
girl, not more than twelve inches high and it looked like it
was made of bronze with a silvered gown. But it was made of
cast glass. At that moment, Olivia, standing in the half-light,
looked like that girl. No, I thought, I am the one made of glass.
If I were to tip out of the bed onto the floor, I would become
a pile of tiny shards.

"Are you still here?" Olivia asked. "Or have you gone back to Skinner?"

"I'm here," I said. "But I feel as if I'm made of glass, Tap me with that beer bottle and I'll shatter into a thousand pieces."

"Olivia gently touched the cold beer bottle to my stomach again. "Drink this, glass man," she said.

She took my hand and pulled me to my feet. We walked out onto the beach. The water was flat, a rich blue, and the waves lapped gently at the sand.

"Are you a dancer, Michael?" she asked.

"Not a very good one."

She faced me and began to hum a song. "Here." She put one of my hands at her waist and took the other. "Dance with me."

And I found myself dancing with a woman wearing a white shirt. Only a white shirt. She was naked beneath the shirt, and there was a flower in her hair. My feet felt light and she said you're doing well. I concentrated on my feet, but I could not keep the rhythm, and she said, it's all right, I can follow. She sang the song, her voice not much more than a whisper, and her body was like falling water, suspended, and we danced to songs that were from another time. A rush of sound in the late afternoon light, the sea that lapped against the sand, and I felt her body against mine, the warmth of her breasts and the press of her hips. We walked on the beach in the soft air that enveloped us and the sea came to our feet. A stray dog appeared, loping along the edge of the water. It ran to the dunes and back to the water and the evening was almost perfect, light and dark like champagne and red wine and chocolate. But somewhere there was the lingering smell of a man burning. I could not tell which man it was.

Deadly Negatives is a **Caravel Book**, a mystery imprint of **Pleasure Boat Studio: A Literary Press**. Following are our other Caravel Books.

The Dog Sox ~ Russell Hill ~ $16 ~ Nominated for an Edgar Award

Music of the Spheres ~ Michael Burke ~ $16

Swan Dive ~ Michael Burke ~ $15

The Lord God Bird ~ Russell Hill ~ $15 ~ Nominated for an Edgar Award

Island of the Naked Women ~ Inger Frimansson, translated from the Swedish by Laura Wideburg ~ $18

The Shadow in the Water ~ Inger Frimansson, translated from the Swedish by Laura Wideburg ~ $18 ~ Winner of Best Swedish Mystery 2005

Good Night, My Darling ~ Inger Frimansson, translated from the Swedish by Laura Wideburgg ~ $16 ~ Winner of Best Swedish Mystery 1998 ~ Winner of Best Translation Prize from *ForeWord Magazine* 2007

The Case of Emily V. ~ Keith Oatley ~ $18 ~ Commonwealth Writers Prize for Best First Novel

Homicide My Own ~ Anne Argula ~ $16 ~ Nominated for an Edgar Award

Orders: Pleasure Boat Studio books are available by order from your bookstore, directly from our website, or through the following:

SPD (Small Press Distribution) Tel. 800-869-7553, Fax 510-524-0852
Partners/West Tel. 425-227-8486, Fax 425-204-2448
Baker & Taylor Tel. 800-775-1100, Fax 800-775-7480
Ingram Tel. 615-793-5000, Fax 615-287-5429
Amazon.com or **Barnesandnoble.com**

Pleasure Boat Studio: A Literary Press
201 West 89th Street
New York, NY 10024
Tel/Fax: 888-810-5308
www.pleasureboatstudio.com / pleasboat@nyc.rr.com